THE CORNFIELD AT NIGHT

The night was still, and colder, the chill of pre-winter with the sharp bite of a hard apple. Dry cornstalks crackled beneath his feet. Nearby, amidst the lights of Orangefield, he heard a dog howl mournfully, hungry or afraid.

The moon was sinking above the corn to his left, off the path he had found, making everything whiter, colder....

Why had he come here, this was madness—

He heard something rustle in the stalks to his left, off the path. He stiffened, waiting for a cold breeze to brush his face. But the corn stalks were perfectly straight, unbowed.

"Hello."

The wet whisper brushed his ear at the moment a dry arm was thrown around his shoulder. He felt heat, and saw the glow of the orange face between himself and the cornfield. It had stepped swiftly out of the ranks—

Petrified with fear, Corrie turned to look into the pumpkin face inches from his own. He felt heat from the candleless glow within; saw wet seeds adhering to the scraped inside of the head, through the sharply etched nose, eyes, smiling mouth.

The scarecrow laughed, pulled him closer with boneless fingers....

Other *Leisure* books by Al Sarrantonio:

TOYBOX

HALLOWS
EVE

AL SARRANTONIO

LEISURE BOOKS NEW YORK CITY

To my sister Theresa

LEISURE BOOKS ®

October 2004

Published by

Dorchester Publishing Co., Inc.
200 Madison Avenue
New York, NY 10016

ISBN 0-8439-5175-3

Printed in the United States of America.

Visit us on the web at www.dorchesterpub.com.

HALLOWS EVE

Chapter One

Any train ride through any town, any October.

The soothing clack of the rails almost had him asleep. His newspaper lay crumpled in the empty seat beside him; the lights in the train car had flickered off in the middle of the sports page and he finally gave up, leaning back against the stiff headrest and turning to watch the night outside. They were passing endless cornfields under a mounting harvest moon; under the strong white light the stalks looked dry as paper, stiff as soldiers at attention.

Something caught his eye ahead in the field of corn, towering above it—an orange and yellow shape that resolved itself into a scarecrow topped by a pumpkin head. As they drew abreast of the figure a fire ignited behind the triangle eyes, the sickle mouth, and it turned its head to look at him. As the train left it behind, he watched the scarecrow move one of its long arms to point directly at him.

1

Did you dream that? Corrie Phaeder asked himself.

Did you dream any of it? Or was it real?

As always, he found that he had no answer.

And now he was back.

As the train slowed into the station, he gave an involuntary shudder at the sight of the sign on the platform.

He had promised himself that he would never come back. And here he was: gathering his things together—his suitcase from the overhead rack, his camera bag—and standing as the train hissed to a stop, and walking to the end of the car and stepping down from the train.

The air was noticeably colder than it had been in New York City that afternoon.

It smelled like Autumn up here, cold as the chilled edge of a knife.

It always had—sometimes even in the middle of summer.

He gave another involuntary shudder, and stood looking at the sign as the train huffed into life behind him and pulled slowly away. There were cold fingers of air on his back at the sudden emptiness behind him.

The sign said:

ORANGEFIELD.

He had a feeling in the deepest, coldest part of him that he would never leave here again.

At least not alive.

* * *

"Need a taxi, kid?"

At the sound of another voice he broke out of his reverie as if waking from sleep. He turned around.

The older, still grizzled face of Jeff Luney regarded him.

"Kid, you been standing there for five minutes staring at that sign, and I doubt it's gonna change. You need a lift somewheres?"

Luney's voice trailed off, and he was looking at Corrie with new interest.

"Don't I know you, kid?"

"Corrie Phaeder," Corrie said, holding out his hand and trying to smile.

"Jeez if it ain't! My God—the Phaeder kid!"

Luney bounded forward and took Corrie's hand in his own. "I'll be damned! We thought we'd never see you again! Bigshot photographer and all, making the big bucks on the west coast—"

Luney suddenly became self conscious, and dropped Corrie's hand. He rubbed his own hand on the side of his pants.

Corrie turned to look at the sign again.

"Guess I'll be staying a while," he said, just barely loud enough to hear.

The ride through town to the Rainer Hotel was about what Corrie expected. Everything looked pretty much as it had when he left: Main Street with the courthouse and shops, Rainer Park.

"Guess you'll be opening up the old house, now

3

that you're back?" Luney said from the front seat. He hadn't stopped talking since they got in the cab, pointing out things he said had changed but which looked just the same to Corrie.

"I'll be talking to Mrs. Williams tomorrow," Corrie answered.

"Strange how it's been empty all these years," Luney went on.

Nothing strange about it, Corrie thought. *I tried to run away, and now I'm back*.

"Gee, you think you'll be picking up with your old pals, Corrie?" They were stopped at a light, and Jeff turned around with his arm resting on the front seat. He had a hungry, expectant look on his face.

The man eats gossip, Corrie thought. *Nothing's changed*.

He thought of what to say, since Luney's next forty passengers would know all about it, and then said, "Maybe."

"Hey, I bet Jerry Bayhill will wanna see you, and Pete Morritz, and the other guys from high school— you hung around them, right? Boy, that Bayhill had one hell of an arm, could throw a football . . ."

The light changed, but Luney continued to stare expectantly at Corrie. The street was empty, here at eleven thirty; Corrie had no doubt that the cabbie would not budge until he was given something.

"And how's about Kathy Marks? You heard there was some trouble with her last year, right? Didn't you used to go with her for a while?"

Kathy Marks.

4

He hadn't thought of that name in more than ten years. Yes, he had dated her for a while . . .

The light had turned red again.

"Sure," Corrie said, forcing a smile onto his face. "I'll look them all up. All the old gang."

"Atta boy," Luney said, pleased with some small victory in the gab wars. He turned around and looked at the red light.

"Damn lights don't ever change around here!" He laughed. "Ain't it great to be back home, kid? And Halloween's on the way!"

Corrie watched Jeff Luney's cab, orange and white, with its broken left tail light (hadn't it always had a broken left tail light?) pull away from the curb. Luney waved back and then gunned the engine.

In a few moments, Corrie was alone on the sidewalk.

There was a particular stillness to the night, which, despite the chill, felt almost like summer. It was a hush, like an indrawn breath. The only sound was the faint click and buzz of the light over the Rainer Hotel entrance, the product of a neon light on the verge of an unattained extinction making the 'H' in Hotel blink on and off. Besides that, there was no other sound.

Corrie looked at the two bags at his feet, one filled with the tools of his trade and the other with all the clothes he owned, and he thought, *Pick them up, start walking, and don't stop until you're back in California.*

He still felt like he was in a dream, one which had started with his screwing up the Mayfair shoot and continuing with Monica walking out (for real, this time, and for good) and then with a week of pills and booze and whatever else he could freeload.

And then . . .

Finding himself on a plane heading east, then a train heading north, and then that sign.

ORANGEFIELD.

Pick them up. Walk away from here. Go back to your other life.

Knowing that was impossible, he picked up the two bags and walked, feeling like a condemned man, into the Rainer Hotel.

Two hours later, after a shower, and after emptying half a fifth of scotch, he almost felt ready for sleep. The scotch helped a little, but not much, and, with a tiny flicker of hope born of alcohol, it occurred to him that maybe he would not dream the dreams that were real, now that he was here.

He had two more fingers of Scotch, capped the bottle, turned out the light and crawled between the sheets.

Let's find out.

Chapter Two

Bill Grant heard something in the night.

What the hell is it now, you old fart?

He sat up carefully in bed, to keep from waking Rose. She was a worse sleeper than he was, blamed it on being the wife of a cop like she did everything else these days.

"Twenty years of waiting for something bad to happen," was how she put it.

Plenty bad had happened, but he always came home.

But lately . . .

There it was, that itch again. Grant now knew what he had heard—it hadn't been anything outside. It had been that little voice in his head, the one he called his 'gut voice' telling him that something bad was going to happen.

It had helped him out for all his years as a uniformed, and then a detective, but this time it was ringing like a claxon, with nothing in sight, which drove him crazy.

Come on out and let's get to it, he thought.

Don't hide—show me who you are.

In answer, there came a slight ruffling of the curtains in the chill breeze.

Groaning softly, knowing that 'Mr. I.', his term for insomnia, which assaulted him every once in a while, was here for the rest of the night, he got out of bed and slid the window closed. Outside there was a tired moon sinking in the west; it made his small backyard, with its fruit trees and trimmed hedges, look black and white.

In the half light, he searched for his slippers, found and put them on, and quietly left the bedroom.

There was a night light in the hallway, the result of one of Rose's constant fears: that they would be attacked in their house. Bill sighed. In the living room there was another of the damned lights, and from the kitchen there emanated a soft green glow, induced by the weird neon-edged clock Rose had bought at a yard sale. She had claimed she liked its cheery large face—but Grant had supposed it was for the prodigious amount of Martian light it gave out at night.

Grant shuffled to the refrigerator and opened the door—its bright white illumination immediately drowned the green glow. There were the last slices of meatloaf that Rose had been saving for his lunch tomorrow—he took them out and made a sandwich, foregoing the brown bag ritual. He'd grab something at Carpy's the next day.

He shuffled back into the hallway, and down the stairs to the basement, which was split into two parts, both belonging to him, the workshop and tv room. No feminine touches here; the walls were covered with paneling and the pictures were of dogs playing poker.

He settled himself into his recliner, put his sandwich on the table next to it and switched on the television.

Nothing on seventy out of seventy-five channels, and then he hit an old John Wayne western. One of the real old ones, before he became a star—

There came a tapping on one of the windows.

Grant stiffened, and immediately went into detective mode:

breeze outside, uncut rose bushes—
intruder—

The house layout rose into his mind—yes, there were uncut rose bushes outside that basement window.

Something tapped at the other window, twenty feet away from the first.

Grant's mental layout of the house was still there—*there was nothing in front of that other window*.

Grant was out of his recliner, his hand already into the side table drawer where he kept his 9mm; the clip was hidden in the back of another drawer underneath and he fumbled it out and inserted it.

Safety off, he moved up the stairs and into the kitchen.

Damned green light—it kept him from getting a good view of the back yard from the window over the sink.

He kept moving to the door to the back yard, and eased it open.

Chill night air and silence.

He edged himself out, cursing the groan of the screen door, which needed to be replaced by the storm door in the garage for the coming winter.

He tried to be quiet, but also cursed the clop of his slippers on the concrete stoop as he descended to the patio.

Nine mm at his side but ready, he moved along the house, stopping at the window where he had heard the second tap—it was bare of bushes, one of Rose's annual plantings having recently given up the ghost.

By moonlight, he saw no footprints in the soft earth.

He moved on, gun raised now, to the other window.

It was choked with thorny rose bushes, with hardly a place for anyone to reach in and tap at the window without pricking themselves.

Movement caught Grant's peripheral vision, and he stood up, looking out over his back neighbor's fence to a small slice of the next street over showing between two houses.

The faintest movement, a flash of orange—

He heard a faint shuffling run, moving away.

Silence.

Far away, a dog barked.

That gut voice, the itch in the back of his head, was still there, but quieter now.

He looked down at the casement window again, frowning.

Something was stuck in the thorn bushes, at the back, near the window.

He reached down and around toward it, and after cursing under his breath at snagging his own hand on a thorn, he brought the prize out.

Before examining it, he paused a moment to suck the blurt of blood from the tiny puncture wound.

He held his hand up toward gray moonlight, studying what he had.

He turned it over—long and thin, not a strip of cloth like he'd thought, stiffer, more like paper.

Giving up on the light of the moon, he carried it into the kitchen, clopping up the back stoop and letting the screen door bang behind him.

Instantly, a neighbor dog began to bark.

There was something: he hadn't heard any dog barking after the window tapping . . .

Not even attempting to study his piece of evidence by the green light of the clock, he snapped on the overhead light, flooding the kitchen with white illumination and blinding himself momentarily.

His puncture wound still bled, and without thinking he passed the long dry thing to his other

11

hand while he sucked the wound dry again. His eyes were on the thing he had found.

It was something dry and curled, yellowed green—

A dry leaf of corn husk.

Chapter Three

Black.
  No dreams.
  Corrie Phaeder woke up, strangely exhausted for a man who had just slept ten hours straight. He was on his back, in the same position as when he had closed his eyes. It was as if a moment had blinked by, and the world had fast forwarded from dead of night to noon, and he had not slept at all.

He felt as if he were filled with lead, clammy, unclean. He remembered then that he had taken a half bottle of scotch, his sleeping pill of choice, and then basically passed out.

The hotel digital clock said it was 12:15.

He tried to remember: when was he supposed to see Mrs. Williams at the real estate office? He thought it was twelve, which meant he was late. He fumbled in his mind files for her number and came up empty; he had it written down somewhere . . .

Yawning, he brought himself into a sitting position on the bed. The room smelled stale. He eyed his suitcase dully—did he have the piece of paper somewhere in there with his clothes, or in his camera bag, or stuffed into the pocket of his jeans . . . ?

He gave up thinking, and eyed the nightstand next to the bed. Under the phone was a slot with a local phonebook in it . . .

Still yawning, he fumbled through the yellow pages to the listings for *Real Estate Brokers* and found nothing under Williams. He forced his mind to work for a moment . . .

Nash & Williams, that was it.

He dialed the number, and naturally got Brenda Nash instead of Lucy Williams.

"Got a pen, hon?" Nash said in an annoying chirp. "I'll give you her cell—"

Corrie groped on the night table, found the hotel ballpoint and the notepad beneath it.

"Go ahead."

Nash chirped a number at him, and Corrie wrote it down.

He hung up the phone before the niceties were finished, and dialed the new number.

Four rings, and then a business-like: "Lucy Williams."

He told her who he was, sat dully through her short lecture about punctuality, and arranged to meet her at her office at four o'clock.

When she started in on another lecture, he said

as politely as he could muster, "I'll be there," and hung up the phone.

He could imagine her stuffing the cell phone back into her huge bag filled with papers, shaking her head . . .

He lay back down on the bed, devoid of any form of energy, and closed his eyes—

When he awoke again on his back, after more blackness and no dreams, it was nearly four o'clock.

"*Shit.*"

He felt even clammier than before, but forced himself from the bed and into the same clothes he had worn the day before. He tried to remember if there was a clean shirt in his bag, but gave up, forcing the old one on and buttoning it. His sports jacket smelled like scotch and cigarettes, but he pushed his arms through the sleeves.

Down the stairs of the hotel, past the desk, into the street . . .

Afternoon sunshine hurt his eyes; it was colder than he thought.

He reached the real estate office at 4:04, and she was just leaving, her car keys in her right hand.

She glared at him, was thinking, Corrie could tell, of telling him he was too late—

"I'm awfully sorry," he forced himself to say, "I just got back from Los Angeles late last night . . ." He forced a winning smile onto his face.

"Two minutes," she said, glancing at her watch and turning back into the office.

"That's all I'll need."

*   *   *

He showed his driver's license, signed a paper, and was given the key to his mother's home.

"All these years, empty," Lucy Williams was saying. "There were a hundred times I could have sold—"

"Thanks for your help," he said, getting up.

She was suddenly solicitous, almost sweet: "Now, Corrie, if you ever decide to sell—"

He waggled the house keys as he walked out the door, not turning around.

"I'll certainly remember you, Lucy," he said.

His feet carried him towards home.

In the 1940s his father returned from World War II and, with the help of a G.I. mortgage and his life savings, as well as those of his wife, built a house along the Sagett River, one of the numerous small feeders in the Adirondack area which eventually spit into the mighty Hudson. The Sagett had only crested once, in 1970, when Corrie was a baby—he remembered the water lapping at the front porch, as close as it got to the house, and sailing a boat in what had been the front yard. The rest of the time the river was only background noise, and a source of occasional swimming, when it was high enough in the summer, which it often was not, and frustrating fishing expeditions.

There were only two other houses on Sagett River Road, both of them much grander than the

Phaeder house, which had two floors and a basement but a gravel drive in place of a garage, which by then his father could not afford. He had bought every close acre of property he could along with the house plot, intending to grow pumpkins, which in the 1950s was a fairly new thing in Orangefield. Ten years later, when Orangefield became the best known town on the East Coast for pumpkins, it would have made him a rich man. But he had no aptitude for farming, and soon went bust. The plots which would have made him rich were sold off to pay mounting debts. Corrie had never heard of him being a success at anything, except bearing a son, which he did late in life. And then he had died. Corrie only remembered him as a furrowed, frowning face staring down at him in his crib.

But his second wife, who bore Corrie at the age of thirty, managed, some way or other, to get along. Corrie never wanted for anything, and he knew from an early age that his mother, a strong woman, would do just about anything for him.

And also, that she never wanted him to leave Orangefield.

Down Main Street a good mile, across Main and then a left onto Potter Street and then toward the river. Most of the housing in Orangefield in the fifties had been developmental, on the other side of town. Here at the western edge, near the river, with the jungle of oak and maple trees, it almost felt Southern.

Corrie could hear it, now—the faint, playful tinkle of the river that had been the background noise to his life for eighteen years.

And then a right turn onto Sagett River Road. It and the river were named after Col. James Sagett, a hero of the Civil War and one of Orangefield's early settlers; his own house, the grandest along the river, was the first Corrie passed, and it looked the same: a plantation house (it was said that Sagett brought the plans back from Chattanooga), and the only one in the entire town that refused to take part in Orangefield's Halloween festivities, even to the point of barring the door to trick-or-treaters. There were many egg-marks around the front door, and Corrie had once beat up Jimmy Sagett III, after the smaller boy had called his mother a name.

And then the Barron house, and then . . .

Home.

He thought he would feel something—anything—when he finally stood before it again. He felt his hand on the house key in his pocket, but that was all. It looked the same: the gravel drive, now ingrown with weeds, leading to the shed in the back, which was missing one door; the front porch, jutting out, painted in peeling white paint (how many times he had repainted that porch with his mother!), the big picture window on the left, the red front door, the neat row of windows on the second floor, the faded white shingles, the single peaked gable over his bedroom on the left, the chimney which ran down to the living room behind it . . .

It was just a house—the house he'd grown up in. *Home.*

His hand tightened around the key in his pocket.

Already he could feel the urge to walk forward, mount the creaking front steps to the white porch, put the key (how his fingers knew that key in his pocket, every worn curve, the one raised rough bit of metal near its key ring which rasped against his fingertip) into the lock and hear the tumblers fall into place, the snick of the house letting go, opening to him . . .

His mother had never lived an uneasy day in it, his father, who had built it partly with his own hands, left no record of trouble with the house itself. No guests had ever complained of anything but perhaps discomfort, in the days before air-conditioning, when the second floor, and especially the tiny third floor storage garret over Corrie's room, became unbearably hot (his father had not provided for cross ventilation in his house plan).

The key was warm in Corrie's hand.

He took a step forward, and then another, and found himself at the front porch.

The line of the Sagett River flood of 1978 was still visible, a faint trace in the overgrowth that

19

marked a spot just along the front of the house; when the river receded it had left a slightly higher grade of silt and soil behind in its retreat.

He had sailed a boat, and been happy, and was five years old then. He remembered the sailboat, a real wooden one, painted blue with a real cream colored linen sail, from a toy store in New York City, slipping away from his fingers and the wind taking it immediately, out over where the road had been (dirt then, paved now) and toward the real river. He had rushed after it, finding himself in water up to his knees and then his mother called him back. He had watched with tears in his eyes as the boat slid away, down into the rushing Sagett and downstream toward, he imagined, the deep roar of the Hudson River.

"I'll get you a new one," his mother had soothed, and she had, but the river had receded by then.

That night he cried in his bed, and thought it was the worst day of his life.

Two years later, he knew how foolish he had been.

Corrie found himself in front of the red door, putting the key into the lock.

He opened the door, and felt something almost whisper *Yesssss*, as the air of the closed-up place was let out.

He stepped in, feeling his hand go cold on the key, still in his fingers.

Home.

Only for him.

Even at the age of seven, he knew he would die here.

Chapter Four

Detective Grant looked through the papers on his desk with indifference. If he loved the job, he hated the paperwork, and there seemed to be more of it all the time. He was old enough to remember the days of carbon copies, and everything in triplicate. He had been one of the few in the department to welcome the coming of the computer, figuring it would free them from all that.

He'd been wrong—and he usually wasn't wrong.

All computers had done was make more paper. Now everything was in quintuplet, and spit out of a printer, which often jammed, or ran out of its ink cartridge, or just plain busted.

And unlike those old triplicate carbons, where everything was attached until you tore off the copies yourself, the five copies the printer spit out tended to get scattered, which meant you had to go back, wait in line, and make *more* copies.

Grant stared at the four copies of a report (b&e, Fowler St., Jeremy Gates, age 17, found with a crowbar outside the residence of one Mr. Jellick; Gates had managed to get the crowbar, and his arm, stuck under the sill of Mr. Jellick's very powerful automatic garage door. One thing that never changed about perp kids: they were stupid) and looked at the line of two uniforms in front of the single department printer. There were three uniforms milling around the copier, which seemed to be broken, giving off a hiccuping sound.

He scowled: how many times had he ended up going to Wilson's Pharmacy, down the block, and inserting his own quarter into Wilson's pay copy machine, just to avoid that line?

He went into his pocket to see if he had any change, and to pull out his cigarette pack.

"Weren't you quitting?" Pell Simpson, the only other detective on the Orangefield police force, asked with a laugh. It was more of a snort.

"I quit every week," Grant answered. "At least my name's not Pelletier, right?"

It was an old routine, and Simpson snorted again. He sat on the edge of Grant's desk, grinning; Grant knew he was counting the four pages Grant held, which told him everything he needed to know about Grant's day. Simpson was tall and lean and stooped, with large feet and a chiseled face and thinning sandy hair. He looked more like a pumpkin farmer than a cop, and was known as "Farmer" when fun wasn't being made of his first name. He kept to himself too much, which had always vaguely bothered Grant, but he was good at his job and pleasant enough.

"Say, Farmer," Grant began, before being cut off by the loud voice of Chip Prohman, the desk sergeant. Prohman was loud and fat and pretty much stupid, at least in Grant's eyes. Grant imagined he would never get any farther than he was now (he'd been a disaster as a beat cop), and would probably end up on the night desk down the road, which would pretty much bury him.

"Hey Grant!" Prohman shouted. No one turned toward him but Bill.

Prohman laughed, a hooting sound. "Here's one for ya! Didn't you mess with a guy named Willims one year, 'round Halloween?"

Grant went instantly through his memory file: *Willims* . . .

By a split-second, Prohman beat Grant's mind: "Bee keeper, wasn't he? Well, he's *dead*! Dispatcher got a call a little while ago. Patrol car just called it in—he *hung* himself! Pretty funny, eh?"

Prohman was grinning ear-to-ear. With barely contained disgust, Grant turned away, and then turned back.

"Where?" Grant asked.

"Where *what*?" Prohman, ever unsharp, blinked back.

"Where did Willims hang himself?"

Prohman rifled through a stack of papers on his desk; his mind had already moved on. Finally he traced his fingers down a particular page, mouthing the words to himself as he read.

"Here it is! Hung himself from a tree in his own backyard! Right next to a hornet's nest! Hey, that's pretty funny—bee guy hanging himself, just like a hanging nest! *Ha*!"

Farmer, frowning, said, "Wasn't that the guy involved with that writer and his wife dying?"

"Kerlan," Grant answered, nodding. "Weird shit. Willims was the guy the D.A. told to keep his yap shut." He looked up at Farmer. "Me, too."

Farmer nodded, got up, stretched his long body. "Well, I've got a line to stand in," he said, and moved off, scooping a handful of his own papers from his desk and moving toward the copy machine.

"Hey, Grant!" Prohman's annoying voice cut through the quiet again. He had another sheet of paper in his hand, and was smiling hugely.

Rather than listen to the desk sergeant's idiotic musings long distance, Grant got up and approached the front desk.

He waited patiently while Prohman mouthed words.

"*Ha*!" the desk sergeant said finally. His smile widened. "Here's a *real* killer for ya! Charley Morton's dead, too!"

Something resembling ice chilled Grant for a moment, and froze him when Prohman went on, hooting: "And get this! Dropped dead in his driveway! And the hospital says it was from . . ."

Prohman leaned closer to the paper, trying to pronounce a word: ". . . anaphylactic . . . shock. From a *hornet*!"

Prohman dropped the paper and gave a huge laugh. "Same day! The bee keeper dies, and the D.A. is killed by a hornet! Whoo!"

Grant was already out the door.

Orangefield was full of weird shit. Grant knew that intimately by now. Especially around Halloween. Even when Grant was a kid, growing up in neighboring Lewiston, everyone had told stories about Orangefield. For a while, even after he joined the Orangefield police force, after being recruited by Riley Gates, he thought it was all talk, jealousy for a town that had made it financially. For Orangefield was nothing if not a gold mine. Best pumpkins in the country, and it was no joke. They grew everywhere, up hillsides and down, in every free plot of ground and every patch and farm. And they grew perfect and fat and with dollar signs pinned to their stems. People drove two hundred and fifty miles just to buy pumpkins in Orangefield, and to partake in the hooey (in Grant's eyes) of the Pumpkin Days Festival, a week-long carnival that brought out the greed and civic pride (often the same thing) in everyone in town. There were endless celebrations, parades, exhibits, tent shows, concerts, speeches, and, for the police, endless trouble.

But it all seemed to work, year after year, and

the town, because of it, was fat and happy, with good schools, a good budget, clean streets, happy citizens . . .

But the *weird shit*—

Grant had believed none of it, at first. Every year around Halloween, as the cash registers began to sing, the farmers' smiles grew wider and the mayor's speeches more full-of-it, something strange, often off in a corner, would happen. Some break-in that couldn't be solved, indeed looked more like a locked-room mystery story than anything else. Or a report of a ghost by a staunchly reliable citizen. Or the burning to black of a huge pumpkin field, someone's entire yearly income, with no source of fire—gasoline, kerosene, *blowtorch*—found by the arson guys. (That was a truly strange one.) Little things. Medium things.

And then, last year: Peter Kerlan, the children's book writer, and his wife.

That had been the strangest, so far.

Grant and Fred Willims, the now-dead bee keeper, had arrived in Kerlan's back yard on Halloween night in time to see the author yank open the door to his wooden tool shed—out stumbled what looked to Grant (and Willims) to be a human skeleton completely covered in hornets. The skeleton stumbled into Kerlan and then the hornets were on him, leaving the skeleton to collapse into bones.

Kerlan was stung to death.

The skeleton had been his wife.

She had been trapped in the shed with a huge hornets nest.

Weird shit.

And here it came again . . .

Grant walked quickly to his car.

He had no trouble finding the bee keeper's house; he had visited Willims once (long after the D.A., Morton, had sealed the case and warned them both never to say anything about it). By then, Willims had started to drink, and told Grant about being bothered.

"It's the hornets," he said. "You think you know how they'll react—hell, there's only one way they *can* react! They react to light—if you shine a flashlight on 'em in the dark, they'll go for it.

"But lately, they've been acting strange—stinging when there's no reason, going for me when there's no light at all, leaving the nest at night—that's something they *never* do! At dusk, they're all in the nest. But not now . . .

"Hell, I found an active nest last winter! You've got to understand, a hornets nest just doesn't make it through the winter. All the workers die, only a couple of females, who become queens, protect themselves somewhere and re-emerge in the spring to start new nests. But on Christmas Eve I found a nest inside a closet in my house, when I went in to pull out some presents I stored there.

"That just doesn't happen!"

* * *

Willims's house was small and tidy—at least it had been. When Grant pulled into the long dirt drive-way he was struck by the condition the house was in—in the short months since he had last seen the bee keeper the house was a shambles—tidy lawn dug up, eaves sagging, two holes in the red shingle roof, a broken window. The front door was open, and had what looked like an axe embedded in it.

Grant parked behind the police cruiser already there. He was immediately approached by a young uniform who started to tell him he had to leave until he recognized Grant.

"Oh, hello, detective."

Grant acknowledged him with a short wave. "What the hell happened here?"

The uniform shrugged. "Beats me. Looks like a war zone. House is all torn up. There are empty honey combs out back—there's no honey in 'em and looks like they haven't been used in a while. But that's not the strangest thing."

"I heard about him hanging himself next to a hornets nest—"

The uniform was grinning lopsidedly. "Stranger than that . . ."

Grant heaved himself out of the car.

"Let's have a look, Jerry."

The uniform turned and led him around the back of the house. They passed what indeed looked like very old honey combs, their doors open on rusted hinges. When Grant had been out here last they had been full of humming happy bees making honey, and had looked almost brand new.

There was a grove of trees beyond the lawn. They made their way toward it, avoiding numerous holes in the ground. Grant stopped to look into one of the ditches and saw a few sluggish insects that looked like small bumblebees moving around at the bottom.

"All the holes are full of 'em," the uniform explained. "We called it in, and Jack Phillips back at the station looked it up on the internet. They're ground nesting bees."

Grant looked up from the hole and counted twenty others, just in their vicinity. The entire yard was filled with them.

"Let's see him," Grant said.

They approached the trees, and the uniform stopped. "Pretty gruesome," he warned. "And *really* strange."

"Stranger than this?" Grant said, indicating the back yard, the wrecked house.

The uniform nodded.

They went into the grove, and immediately the hairs on the back of Grant's neck stood on end. A roiling, hissing sound got incrementally louder. Ahead of them the trees thickened, and he saw an aluminum ladder propped up against one in particular.

Something brushed past Grant's ear and he swatted it away.

Al Sarrantonio

They reached the ladder, and Grant looked up. A body was hanging limp, back to him, a dried stain down one pant leg. Red and gold leaves, not yet fallen, hid most of the head and the branch to which the rope was tied.

Grant moved to the other side to look at the face. *"Jesus."*

"Didn't I tell you?"

Grant turned away for a moment, bile rising into his throat. He hadn't thrown up on the job in ten years. But this . . .

A good portion of the upper part of Willims's face was gone; his eye sockets were cleaned of flesh, showing white bone and two gaping dark holes. The head was canted to one side, the tongue stuck thickly out.

In and out of the eye holes and mouth crawled hornets, which were transporting between Willims's head and a huge nearby hanging paper nest. He watched one insect take off from the bee keeper's face, make the short journey, and then land at the bottom of the hole, crawl into the opening at the bottom and disappear.

"What the—"

Grant's eye was drawn to what looked like a second nest in the same tree nearby—it was haloed by hornets like a cloud. There was a third in a neighboring tree, and then another, and another . . .

All of the trees around them were burdened with hornet nests, two or three to each, hanging like ripe fruit.

The air above them was filled with a fog of hornets.

"Let's get the hell out of here," Grant said.

The uniform didn't hesitate to follow him out. "Got to tell you, detective, at first I didn't want to go in there. Just had me a peek. But a peek was enough."

The hum of hovering insects retreated.

"You can go if you want," Grant said.

The uniform nodded. "No problem. You gonna stay?"

"Just for a little while. I knew this guy. If you haven't already, tell the coroner to get out here, and tell him to bring a couple of insect experts with mosquito netting and equipment with him."

"Right-o."

They stepped around holes and the uniform went to his car and got in, while Grant headed for the house.

He didn't know what he was looking for, if anything. He didn't feel as if he owed Willims anything in particular. It was more wanting to understand what the hell was going on.

Weird shit.

He entered the house through the open front door, briefly examining the axe, and immediately the hairs on his neck stood up again. It felt like there was electricity in the air. The place was a shambles, and dark; he flipped on the nearest light switch but nothing happened.

His shin hit an overturned coffee table; there

were broken pieces of chairs, and the sofa's stuffing was pulled out in bunches.

Grant examined the sofa: there were insects of some kind crawling around the holes.

The kitchen had been trashed, the single bathroom, the hallway filled with torn books and broken dishes; something nailed to the wall with a railroad spike that proved to be a recent copy of the Orangefield *Herald*. The headline on the first page proclaimed "Pumpkin Days Coming!" and showed a happy first-grader holding a pumpkin nearly as big as he was.

There was something scribbled on the wall next to the paper in what looked like blood. On closer examination Grant determined that it was kitchen fat scooped from an open coffee can which lay on the floor on its side.

In big bold letters it read: SAMHAIN.

Grant remembered Samhain from the Kerlan case—he was the Celtic Lord of the Dead who supposedly brought them back to life on Halloween— Kerlan had written a children's book called *Sam Hain and the Halloween That Almost Wasn't*.

Samhain had supposedly brought Kerlan's dead wife's skeleton, covered in hornets, back to life . . .

Again something brushed by Grant's ear, and he swatted it away—then thought of D.A. Charley Morton, who had just died of anaphylactic shock from an insect sting.

Grant gave an involuntary shudder as something else brushed by his ear, his face.

He was standing outside an open door blocked with broken furniture. He became aware that a sound had been building all along, a hissing hum like the one he had heard in the grove of trees outside.

He tried to peer through the blockage, but the pieces had been fit together so exactly that he could not see into the room beyond, which he guessed to be Willims's bedroom.

He pushed at the base of a lamp, which was fitted into the hole like a puzzle piece. It fell off into the room and hit the floor with a clatter.

He only had a peek—a cloud of hornets outlined by light from the window, almost too thick to see through; the ceiling bulging down into the room, broken apart like the burst skin of a gas-filled bag, a huge, bulging paper hornets nest, some five feet in diameter, hovering just inches over the unmade bed—

He backed away, gagging, and stumbled his way out of the house, barking his shin on the same broken coffee table as he did so.

He stood gasping for air in front of the house; saw in his peripheral vision that a cloud of something from the grove of trees was moving his way.

Behind him, in the gloom of the house, the hissing sound was building.

Again he swatted something from his face; and again.

He stumbled to his car, got in, closed the window.

The two clouds, one from the house, one from the tree grove, were merging, building like a tornado.

He threw his keys into the ignition, rammed the car into drive and kicked dirt turning it around and tearing down the driveway to the main road.

He didn't stop breathing heavily till he was halfway back to town, checking his rearview mirror all the way.

Weird shit.

Very weird shit.

Chapter Five

Corrie Phaeder awoke from another black sleep. It was as if someone had thrown a switch, taking him from slumber to wakefulness.

Where am I?

For a moment, he had no idea. It was dark, and smelled close and stuffy, and his hand, when he reached it out, hit something solid that he didn't recognize.

For a second he thought he was back in L.A., at a friend's house after Monica kicked him out—

Then he thought he was in the Rainer Hotel—

Then—

Home.

He knew the place now; knew it in the dark or light. He was prone on the living room sofa, the Sheridan that his mother had re-upholstered twice while he was growing up. It had originally been a wine color, and he remembered being sick on it when he was little, with a blanket over him while he sweated out a fever . . . then it had been a golden yellow, which his mother had loved in a swatch but hated when the entire piece of furniture was done . . . then, finally, it was a red embroidered fabric, which it was now . . .

There was a familiar pillow under Corrie's head. How long had he slept . . . ?

He sat up, feeling as sluggish as he had before he closed his eyes. *Like no sleep at all.* He looked at the picture window facing him, what must be gray moonlight drifting in, illuminating the dust motes in the air.

He fumbled to his right, the tall brass lamp with a silk shade, his fingers under the shade, twisting the switch.

The room was bathed in soft yellow light.

She always liked 40 watt bulbs . . .

Yawning, stretching, he got up and turned on three other lamps, which merely deepened the yellow glow in the room. All 40-watters . . .

The room was exactly as he had remembered it. Dark mahogany furniture, Victorian style for the most part, with other out-of-date touches. A Tiffany chandelier out in the hallway—he remembered thinking it was magic light when he was little. No carpeting, but dark Persian rugs, tasseled, covered the wood floors. An imposing bookcase guarding the wall next to the opening into the dining room. Another childhood memory: standing on his tip-toes to try to reach Lewis Carroll's *Al-*

ice's Adventures in Wonderland, which was on the third shelf.

He walked over to it now and almost had to bend down to slide it out of its accustomed spot.

A line of dust across the top. He blew it off and it clouded away, briefly forming a shape: an all-too-distinct head of a pumpkin, mouth grinning.

He turned cold—the cloud dissipated into dust motes . . .

Already . . .

The book's faded buckram cover, an inset picture of Alice cowering, surrounded by a whirling pack of cards, one of Tennyson's line drawings which had been tinted.

He opened the book at random. There was another colored Tennyson drawing: the enraged Queen pointing at a composed Alice and screaming "Off with her head!"

He smiled, then the smile froze on his face as the drawing moved.

The picture abruptly deepened, became three dimensional. The Queen turned with her finger still pointing to look straight at Corrie. There was unimaginable fury in her eyes. She straightened her finger at him and screeched, in a piercing high voice: ***"OFF WITH HIS HEAD!"***

Alice, arms folded, turned to regard him with detached interest—

He dropped the book, breathing heavily.

It's starting again.

His eye was drawn to a flash of color. He turned

to the picture window and saw something wink again, redly. The river? No, it was beyond the river.

He quickly turned all the lamps out in the room.

He stood before the picture window, and waited for it to repeat. He could see the river moving blackly under the light of the moon, stunted now by trees which blocked the sinking orb. The water looked like boiling lava. Through a break in the trees on the far bank he saw it again—

A red flash.

Something flaring into life.

It lit, and stayed on.

Not red, but deep orange.

The round head of a pumpkin . . .

He closed his eyes, and then made a map of Orangefield in it.

The cornfield he had passed as the train drew into Orangefield was indeed in that direction.

He opened his eyes again: the orange head glowed brighter.

Corrie closed his eyes, and when he had made up his mind he opened them again and the light in the distance was gone.

Chillier still. Corrie had forgotten what weather and seasons were like in the East—after more than a decade in California, his wardrobe had become almost seasonless. His brown sports jacket was about the heaviest garment he owned—he would have to go to Meager's Sporting Goods tomorrow and buy a fall jacket with a zipper.

He crossed the footbridge a quarter mile down-river, passing to his surprise a new house on River Road. It was well hidden by trees from his own, but the plot was new enough that grass had not yet grown in on the front lawn. It was nicer than the current McMansion style of big house; looked like it had been designed by an architect. A huge farm-house, it somehow looked right. There were lights on in many of the windows, and Corrie heard a childish squeal from the back yard.

The footbridge had been mended somewhere along the way. There were new cedar planks all the way across, and strong thick rope fencing each side. In a way Corrie was disappointed; part of the fun of crossing it when he was young was to see if you or one of your friends would fall in. It had happened a few times, but Sagett River was not wide or dangerous at this point, and a dunking meant little more than a swim to shore while your buddies hooted derisively.

The path through the woods was still there, too, as worn as ever. A carpet of new leaves covering last year's pine needles made it soft as a rug.

Corrie was out of the woods too quickly. He remembered it as being a long and scary walk.

Something else that had been sized down by time . . .

He stood on a small hill, with a breathtaking view in front of him.

The moon was sinking before him, but still cast orange-gray torchlight on a scene from a Brueghel painting. Below him the fields were cut into blocks as if by the hand of God—mostly separate pumpkin fields, bursting with fruit ready to be picked (Corrie thought of the Pumpkin Tender, as he had been known—he wondered if poor Aaron Peters was still doing the job he was known for, which was to take care of the lion's share of pumpkins in Orangefield. The man had an orange thumb) but also the occasional plot of onions (which also grew well in Orangefield's rich black soil) and corn.

Corrie's eye was drawn to the railroad tracks a half mile to his left; he moved his eye up the briefly viewed tracks, until he spied a corn field.

The orange light flashed, a faraway beacon.

Hugging himself, Corrie walked down the hill and headed that way.

The night was still, and colder, the chill of prewinter with the sharp bite of a hard apple. Dry cornstalks crackled beneath his feet. Nearby, amidst the lights of Orangefield, he heard a dog howl mournfully, hungry or afraid.

The moon was sinking above the corn to his left, off the path he had found, making everything whiter, colder . . .

Why had he come here? This was madness—

He heard something rustle in the stalks to his left, off the path. He stiffened, waiting for a cold breeze to brush his face. But the corn stalks were perfectly straight, unbowed.

He heard the rustle again and thought of that dog; he did not like dogs . . .

"Hello."

The wet whisper brushed his ear at the moment a dry arm was thrown around his shoulder. He felt heat, and saw the glow of the orange face between himself and the cornfield. It had stepped swiftly out of the ranks—

"Let's walk, shall we?"

Petrified with fear, Corrie turned to look into the pumpkin face inches from his own. He felt heat from the candleless glow within; saw wet seeds adhering to the scraped inside of the head, through the sharply-etched nose, eyes, smiling mouth.

The scarecrow laughed, pulled himself closer with boneless fingers. It made a dry, ticking sound as it walked—

"You can call me John, if you like."

Corrie, holding his breath, said nothing.

"Be afraid, if you must, but listen to me. You're going to see a lot of me in the next couple of weeks."

The scarecrow stopped walking, his dry stalk fingers digging into Corrie's shoulder to make him halt also. The scarecrow urged him around with his dry fingers until the two of the them were face to face.

43

Al Sarrantonio

The face, though horribly unreal, looked alive.

Corrie felt as if he were going to faint.

The head regarded him squarely.

"I'm not an illusion," John said. When he spoke, his grinning jack o'lantern mouth did not move, but Corrie could nevertheless feel the breath of his speech. "I'm not a dream, even though you think that sometimes your dreams are real. You always have, ever since you were seven years old."

Corrie's mouth was dry, but he managed to say, "Yes."

"They're not dreams. They never were."

Corrie tried to speak, but said nothing. His body was cold as ice.

This has to be a dream. All of it has to be a dream.

"If it makes you feel more at ease," John said, "make believe that you *are* dreaming. That you'll wake up any moment on the Sheridan couch in your mother's house."

"Ever since I was seven—"

"I know," John said, cutting him off. "I'm afraid all that will come back to you. There's no other way. If there was, I wouldn't be here now . . ."

"Who *are* you?" There was a desperation in his voice that Corrie didn't know he possessed.

Corrie swore that the corners of the pumpkin head's smile widened ever so slightly, though they looked as hard and fresh as if they had just been carved. "I told you: call me John."

"Who are *all* of you! Why has this been happening to me! I went to California to get away from you! And now I'm here again, *and I don't know why!*"

There was almost a touch of pity in John's voice. "I'm afraid that can't be helped."

To his own astonishment, Corrie was on his knees and crying. *"What in hell is happening to me!"*

"We could all ask that, couldn't we?" John answered, enigmatically.

For a brief moment, the scarecrow laid a finger on Corrie's shoulder. "Believe me, if there was any other way . . ."

He turned, and began to make his way back toward the rows of corn.

Corrie was still on his knees, weeping. It was as if a dam that had been erected when he was seven years old had suddenly been dynamited.

"It's not fair!"

"When you go home, you can sleep now."

Corrie heard a dry rustle, retreating light steps.

Through a veil of tears, he saw nothing but corn stalks in front of him.

He pounded one fist on the ground, again, again.

"Not . . . fair . . ."

Later, from the hilltop, as he made his way home, he turned to regard the corn field, and saw the figure of the scarecrow, tiny and far away, standing mute and unlit, a dead sentinel.

Chapter Six

"Being a cop's wife I can handle. I always have. *But not this other shit.*"

"I don't want to fight with you again, Rose."

His wife was out of bed, at least. She had her housecoat on, and her cigarette pack out on the kitchen table, next to her cold coffee. Six o'clock in the evening and she had her housecoat on.

"Why don't you get dressed," Grant offered. "We'll go out."

Butting out a spent cigarette in her big frog ashtray (green, huge, a frog on his back with a laughing face and his belly concave to receive ashes), she shook her head emphatically no. "I told you, I don't like to go out."

"We haven't been out in months—"

She turned her fierce, frightened eyes on him. *"No!"*

Grant loosened his tie; this battle was already

lost. He turned away from her, pulling the tie out of his collar and said unenthusiastically, "What about dinner?"

"We'll order in again. From Chow's."

"Chinese *again*?"

"I *like* Chinese!"

Twenty-seven years, and he felt like he hardly knew her. It was like starting all over again, with a stranger.

Knowing the outcome, he decided to try again anyway. He let out a long breath, turned around and sat across the kitchen table from her. She was fumbling another Newport out of the pack, and Grant took one. She scowled at him briefly, then said, "Go ahead."

"Thanks."

He watched her light up, her trembling fingers, darting eyes. Then she concentrated on the cigarette and was fine.

He started off slow, after drawing on his own cigarette. "Don't you think we should maybe try another balance on the meds?"

She became instantly fierce. "*Screw* the meds!"

"You stopped taking them again . . . ?" He tried to keep his voice calm.

"They make me sleepy. And jumpy." She gave a fractional, wry smile. "And depressed."

"They're supposed to help."

"*Well they don't!*"

"Rose." He tried to keep the weariness out of his voice.

When he looked up from the table to meet her eyes she was staring at him fiercely. "You want to send me to that place again? Killborne? Let 'em stare at me through that fisheye glass in the door?"

"I never wanted you to go there the first time. The doctor—"

"Screw the doctor! And screw you!"

She grabbed her cigarettes, swept her matches up and stood, knocking her chair backwards. It hit the floor.

Grant looked down at the table. A few moments later he heard the door to the bedroom close with a bang.

Five hours later he woke up in front of the television, still fully dressed. He looked at the clock on the cable box—it was just after ten. He shifted in the recliner, straightened up, stared at the television. A familiar scene: Clint Eastwood in *Pale Rider*, the hard squinting eyes under the brim of his hat staring at the town going up in flames. Hadn't he been watching this movie when he fell asleep?

He checked the on-screen tv guide and discovered that the movie had immediately been repeated. He was watching the same damn thing all over again.

He aimed the remote at the screen.

"Bang," he said, and the picture went off.

His mouth tasted foul; he eyed the partially empty scotch bottle on the table next to his chair, the glass with a little amber liquid pooled at the bottom. He'd had ice and water, hadn't he? Next to it was the crumpled remains of a tv dinner aluminum tray.

He picked up the glass and drank what was in it.

The hair on the back of his neck stood up a split second before he heard dry tapping on the window.

This time I catch you.

He was out of the recliner in a second, his hand already on the still-loaded 9mm, pulling it out of the drawer.

He was on the stairs and out the back door—

Huffing breath, he saw a dim figure just disappearing over the back yard fence. There was something strange about it . . .

He was after it without thinking.

He couldn't quite vault the fence, which was chain link, but he was over it with a one-foot assist. The figure was running, making an odd flapping sound, just disappearing between two houses.

Plenty of places to hide on the next street . . .

Bill saw it heading to the right, and made a calculated move, cutting over one back yard and then sprinting down the driveway.

He came up short at the curb.

The street was empty.

No—there, on the other side, something was walking, vanishing behind a high hedge.

He ran after it, brought the gun up as a head appeared above the hedge—

"Don't move!"

A startled face: a woman in a bathrobe, a clutch of something that she dropped—

"I forgot to get my mail . . ." she explained, automatically raising her hands.

"I'm sorry," Grant said. He bent to help her retrieve it, then saw movement up the street, out of the corner of his eye—

"Sorry again," he said, and ran after the retreating figure—he could faintly hear that strange, flapping sound.

The figure was a half block away from him, and stretching the distance, when it made a mistake, taking a sudden left turn into the neighborhood playground. Grant smiled to himself; the area, which was flat and grassy with a jungle gym and a single tennis court, was surrounded by a high fence.

I've got you, you bastard.

He pulled in to the entrance moments after seeing the figure go in. His 9mm was up now, and he looked to the left, the right.

He saw nothing.

Dammit.

Then—yes—right in front of him, standing by the jungle gym slide, trying to blend into the night . . .

Grant pointed the gun. "Stay right there," he said. "Don't move a muscle. It's time to talk."

The figure stood still. There was something very odd about the head. And parts of whatever it was wearing were being raised and lowered by the wind—

"Just stand still," Grant ordered.

Twenty feet.

Ten.

That head—?

In the wink of an eye, something happened to the figure. Grant came very close to pulling the trigger of his 9mm. There was a dry sound, and a crack—and suddenly the figure wasn't there.

Grant stood over the spot, wheeling around, waiting for the sound of feet hitting fence, but there was nothing but silence.

Nothing.

He was alone.

Still holding his gun tightly in his right hand, he bent down at the spot where the figure had been.

There was a pile of what looked like dry, bleached leaves inside a sack, and something oddly shaped beside it.

It was an old jacket wrapped around a frayed flannel shirt, a pair of pants with holes in it, all stuffed with dry corn husks.

Beside it was a broken pumpkin, the face still intact, carved as if ready for Halloween. There were wet seeds stuck to the inside, as if it had been freshly prepared.

More weird shit, Grant thought.

Just what I don't need—

The pumpkin face flared into life, as if someone had put a candle behind it. And then, even more strangely, the mouth moved.

"See Corrie Phaeder," it said.

Chapter Seven

In his own bed.

The house was quiet now. For a while, the things in the walls had been scrambling, making noise, and he was afraid that the wall itself would do one of its tricks.

But then, as soon as he climbed into bed, his heart pounding, the house had rested. He could almost hear it give a huge sigh around him, as if happy to have him home.

He had slept for a long while, and had dreamed. It was almost dawn. The curtains were pulled back and he saw faint pink purplish light through the half denuded branches of the oak tree outside his window. The branches moved, and he held his breath, thinking that the tree might be doing one of its tricks.

But it was only the wind.

It was cool in the room. He pulled the quilt up

to his chin, and, as if in answer, the gas burner snapped on in the basement, and the baseboards clicked with expanding heat. He felt a familiar warmth rising next to the bed.

Oddly, he didn't feel the terror he thought he would experience coming back to this room. Remembering his last day here, twelve years ago, he thought he would be gripped with fear . . .

Instead, it was almost as if all was forgiven.

The house sighed around him again, like a cat settling down to a nap.

He looked straight overhead, at the round hatch that let up into the garret. By standing on his bed he would be able to unlock the hatch, pull down the short wooden stairs and climb up . . .

All the warmth from the quilt, the baseboards, bled out of him.

For a brief moment it looked like the hatch was opening by itself, falling down onto him—

And then everything in the room was back to normal.

He yawned, and felt warm again, and, after fighting the urge, closed his eyes.

Then he was asleep, and dreaming again.

He dreamed of Monica, this time. It was the first time she had really pushed herself back into his thoughts since he left L.A.

It was early in their time together, and she was always smiling. He'd done a photo shoot near the beach at Malibu, on the sand but under a cabana, which was logical enough since cabanas were what the advertiser was selling. They had the usual covey of girls in bathing suits, bikinis for the most part but there was one girl in a one-piece black suit that he couldn't take his eyes off of. The camera seemed to love her, too. While she was no different at first glance than the other models, something happened when she smiled—not only her whole face lit up but the entire surrounding area. It was more of a spotlight than a smile, and he was caught in it immediately. That and the one piece suit made her stand out.

He asked her out after the shoot, something he had done a few times before. It had never worked out; usually on the first date, by the second at most, the differences between Corrie and whatever model it happened to be surfaced immediately. More often than not it happened when they opened their mouths to speak: usually, not much came out. When it was obvious there wasn't much beyond me-me-me, Corrie never called for another date. Or vice versa.

But this time it was different, immediately. Monica was not only attractive but intelligent, and she seemed more interested in the world around her than herself. Corrie never heard her utter the word 'me.' It was always, 'How lucky I was to see Naples,' or 'You would love Jamaica, the food is incredible,' or 'We have to go to a Mighty Ducks game—you'll love it!'

"*Why the one piece suit?*" *Corrie asked her on their first date, and she didn't even blush.*

"*Birthmark, and a doozy, right about here.*" *She made a circle, and not a small one, left and above her belly button. "It almost kept me from being a model.*

But, heck, there are plenty of jobs where you don't have to show too much skin, and I only want to do it another year or so anyway. I want to go back to UCLA, to grad school. The modeling's my stash."

She smiled again, lighting up the room, and Corrie found himself falling in love with her on the spot. The long dark hair, the almost perfect features, the dark brown eyes, the slim body, the great legs—he had seen all of this a hundred times, but never quite like this. She made the rest of them look like cartoon characters—as if they had been drawn, not created.

Not on the first date, but on the second, he got to examine the doozy of a birthmark.

And then things had gotten more and more perfect, and Monica had moved in with him while they both continued to work . . .

And then the fight, the one he had started, for no real reason other than that something in his head was telling him to. Even though he tried to fight it, the nasty words came out, and continued to come out.

And then she was gone.

The last thing he saw of her was that smile, when she turned at the door with her suitcase in her hand. It had been just as dazzling, and made his heart skip a beat just as it had the first time he saw it and every time since. But now it was sad and puzzled.

"I don't know why this is happening, Corrie," she

said. "But I believe that things happen for a reason. I hope that what you're doing is worth the end of this—because I thought it would last. Maybe forever.

"I hope you're happy, Corrie—I hope you're happy always . . ."

And then the wonderful smile was erased by tears, and she turned and went out of his life, and he couldn't stop her, couldn't tell her why he was going back home to Orangefield—

He woke up, and heard a bird singing in the oak tree outside his window. The clock said 9:30. The room was dappled with sunlight blinking through the oak branches.

It was bright October outside.

He felt rested.

So now the old pattern is back: I'll dream of my real life during the night in photo-minute detail, dream of things that have really happened to me—and, during the day—

He turned at the sound of something ticking in one corner of the room, which turned into a scrabbling sound up the wall. There was a groan overhead, and the hatch into the garret bulged for a moment, then popped back into its normal shape.

—during the day—

Somewhere below him, deep in the house, he heard a long swishing sound, like a broom being moved in one long stroke against a floor. There was a whispery chuckle which faded into a loud *bang*, like a hammer against a board.

The birdsong abruptly ended. Corrie wondered if it had ever been real. He looked out the window and the window itself had switched from a vertical rectangle to a horizontal one—in a flash it was back the way it should be.

—*during the day I'll live in a nightmare.*

Chapter Eight

Corrie Phaeder!

There was a name Bill Grant hadn't thought of in at least ten years.

And the decade had been better for it.

Corrie Phaeder!

The one who got away!

Grant still got angry when he thought about it.

The kid had killed his own mother, Grant was sure of it.

He had learned over the years that, just as there was such a thing as love at first sight, so too was there such a thing as dislike at first sight. He'd hated the Phaeder kid the first time he laid eyes on him. Instantly. The kid had radiated bad news, and Grant had not only picked up on it but fed off it. It had gotten so bad that the captain at the time, Jim Leersohn, had taken him off the case and put Jerry

Farrow, who was now captain, on it instead.

Which had ultimately resulted in the kid walking away, not only from a murder charge but from Orangefield, too. It had started a rift between Grant and Farrow that had never healed.

And now Corrie Phaeder was back in Orangefield.

Grant couldn't believe it.

He had the kid's case folder open on his desk in front of him, but he didn't even need to look at it. He knew every detail of the case by heart.

The kid had, plain and simple, gotten away with murder.

And what he had tried to do to Kathy Marks, the librarian, was something else that Grant had never been able to prove, and something, to this day, that the librarian would not talk about. Grant was still sure that Riley Gates, his partner at the time, was wrong about that one . . .

The kid had poisoned everything he touched.

And now he was back.

Grant lit a cigarette, flipped the file closed, and got up.

The house looked exactly the same. The stretch of Sagett River Road in front of it was paved now, something it hadn't been back in the early '90s—and if Grant remembered correctly there was a new house next to Phaeder's. But except for that and the weeds and tall grass in the front yard and the peeling paint on the porch, the property looked exactly the same. The door ajar on the shed at the end of the driveway had never been fixed. Grant remembered his first interview with Phaeder, which had taken place right next to that door—

As if on cinematic cue, Corrie Phaeder pushed the broken door aside and emerged from the gloomy interior of the shed, blinking at the sunlight. Shading his eyes, he stared at Grant's car and then at Grant as he got out of it.

Grant swore the kid's squint changed to a frown, and Phaeder turned and went back into the shed.

Grant retrieved his notebook, which, on a case, might as well be attached to his left hand with glue, and a pen from his shirt pocket, and made the long, slow walk up the driveway. He had always liked the crunch of gravel beneath his feet . . .

Phaeder was struggling with the other door, trying to push it out, and gave up as Grant reached him. Instead he angled the broken door down as if the missing lower hinge was there and moved it carefully out and open, pushing it against the left edge of the shed front and blocking it there with a nearby brick. It creaked ominously but stayed.

"Can I help you, Detective Grant?" Phaeder asked in a flat voice, re-entering the shed; he was lost to view in the darkness, rummaging around.

"Just wondering why you're back, Corrie," Grant said, trying to keep any venom from his voice. At first sight of Phaeder in more than a decade he instantly felt the same dislike he'd felt the first time.

"Weren't you told to stay away from me?" Corrie said. He was still in the shadows. "Detective Farrow—"

"He's Captain Farrow," Grant offered. "He's my boss, now. You can call him if you want. I'm sure he'll paste my ears back for coming over here. But I thought someone should."

"Despite what you think, Detective Grant," Phaeder said, walking out of the shadows; he had a paint brush in one hand and screwdriver in the other, "I always liked you. I admired your intelligence." Phaeder's eyes did not avoid his own. "I could never understand why you wouldn't listen to me."

Grant met and held the kid's level stare. "Because you were full of shit."

"If only that was true, detective," Phaeder answered. He put the paint brush and screwdriver down on a drip-covered gallon of paint already on the driveway. As if Grant had left he added, "I have no idea if this paint'll be any good after all this time . . ."

"Why did you come back?" Grant asked. He was aware that his ever-present notebook was open to a blank page, and his pen ready, but that he had written nothing.

Again Phaeder met his gaze. "I wish I could tell you. I certainly didn't want to."

Grant was suddenly overcome with anger, the

thing his mentor Riley Gates had warned him about years ago. He knew what he was doing was wrong, and stupid, but he couldn't help himself. He flipped his notebook closed, jammed it into his coat pocket and jabbed the pen in Corrie Phaeder's direction.

"Because you're lying. Because you lied from the beginning. I remember your bullshit well: 'how your dreams were real and reality your dreams.' They found your mother at the bottom of those stairs stabbed twenty-three times and you were the only one in the house. I don't care if you were in a wheelchair. You killed her."

Phaeder's voice was calm. "I told you then, and I'm telling you now—"

"You killed her, dammit! There was no other way she could die—"

"Wasn't there? Have you ever had anything strange happen to you in this town, detective?"

The question made Grant pause.

Phaeder went on, calmly, as if he were talking to himself. "Have you ever heard a noise you couldn't identify, or seen something you knew couldn't be real, or had something happen that was real but couldn't be? Can you tell me that in all your years in Orangefield, nothing strange has ever happened to you?"

Before Grant could answer he went on: "Well, that's my life, 24/7. That's what I do. And I didn't kill my mother. Please leave me alone, detective."

Phaeder turned his back on Grant, knelt down

in front of the paint can and began to work on it with the screwdriver, trying to pry open the lid.

"Just tell me why you're back in Orangefield," Grant said after a moment. He had his notebook open to the blank page again, but already knew he would write nothing.

"I told you, I don't know. I lost everything to come back here." He turned around to look at Grant with haunted eyes. "And I'd give it all up just to be anywhere else but here."

Grant said, "I'll be watching you," and walked back to his car.

It had not gone the way he wanted it to. He was mad at himself twice—first, for letting the kid control the interview and second, because the kid had thrown him.

Have you ever had anything strange happen to you in this town, detective?

The fact was, he had. And more as time went on. And plenty lately.

Weird shit.

Have you ever had anything strange happen to you?

For the first time since he had first met Corrie Phaeder, he felt he had been able, in the tiniest part, to crawl into the kid's head. Which had really been his problem with the kid all along. He'd never met anyone, guilty or innocent, who wouldn't let him in. And now Corrie Phaeder, with that one look, had let him have a taste.

Have you ever . . . ?

For the first time, he felt he knew something about Corrie Phaeder.

The kid, for some reason, was scared shitless.

Chapter Nine

Corrie met the Bright kid while he was trying to mix the glue that the porch paint had become.

It looked like a trip to Sears after all, before that porch could be painted.

The Bright kid was standing in front of him when he stood up and turned around after all but giving up. Even the addition of a little ancient turpentine hadn't helped.

For the briefest moment he thought it was Detective Grant, either returned in different form or metamorphosed by the house; but then the kid grinned and said, "Hi!"

She waved her hand in a circular motion, her smile widening.

"I'm Regina Bright. Everybody calls me Gina for short though I'd rather be called Reggie but no one will call me that will you call me that?"

Her words came in a rush, and Corrie was instantly reminded of the cartoon character Sniffles the Mouse, who spoke whole paragraphs as one sentence.

"Uh, sure, I'll call you Reggie if you want."

She smiled. She was short with red hair cut in bangs, dressed in painter's pants and a gold tee-shirt. Her blue sneakers were covered with mud.

"You've been playing by the river? Didn't your mother tell you not to do that by yourself?"

Her smile vanished for a moment, then came back. She looked at her shoes. "Yes I guess I shouldn't but there was no one to play with and I wanted to make some mud pies so I went down to the riverbank but not too close and the river isn't rushing by so much today and I didn't get wet just my sneakers got muddy."

"I—"

"My mom told me not to come near you either 'cause something bad happened a long time ago but I wanted to see the haunted house like Bella my friend from school told me and the scary guy who lives in it you don't look so scary are you scary?"

The smile was back; this kid didn't have an ounce of fear in her.

There was a tentative, concerned shout from up the road: "*Gina . . . ?*"

Reggie's smile widened: "That's my mom she'll whack me one if she finds out I've been here so I'm gonna go I'm seven years old how old are you?"

"I'm, uh—"

Again the call of her name, closer, more urgent: "*Geeee-naaa!*"

Reggie turned to run, then stopped. "You can tell me next time I'll sneak over again you look like a nice man aren't you glad to have met me?"

"Uh, yes—"

She was off like a rocket, into the tall weeds across the street. Corrie watched her progress as the weed tops moved with her passing, and she was soon away toward her house, where she would be walloped for playing in the mud, or for going to see the 'scary man.'

Then again, Corrie would put his money on the bet that she was sneaking all the way around her house at this moment, into her back yard, where she would remove her sneakers, creep into the house and up to her room, and pretend that she had been there all along.

It's what he would have done.

Two hours later he was back from Sears with three gallons of white outdoor latex paint, a new brush, and the will to get the porch done.

But the day had clouded over, and he wasn't part of the way through scraping the old peeling paint before it began to rain. The temperature cooled as if someone had suddenly turned on an air-conditioner, and then the rain came down in summer torrents. The wind picked up, and then blew sheets of water at the porch. Corrie could hear the nearby river churning and splashing.

Shivering, Corrie retreated into the house with the paint and tools, which he stacked in the hallway behind the front door. His eyes turned for a brief moment to the bottom of the stairs, the spot where he had found his mother—

The chandelier in the dining room, through an archway to his left, blinked on and off. It was an ornate glass piece, heavy and dusty.

It blinked on again, brightened, then went off.

Corrie ignored it.

The rain was beating at the windows, many of which he had opened, and he moved around the house closing them, starting with the front where the force of the wind was located. It had become very damp and cold in the house.

He stopped in his bedroom to pick up a sweater from his bag, and pulled it on over his head.

The floor moved beneath his feet.

It felt like a wave had rippled across the room—and sure enough, as he watched, the floor—bare wood covered with a braided oval rug in blue and red, began to churn as if it was the Sagett River. The wood turned elastic, throwing up peaked waves, which then rolled toward him.

He was thrown to the floor, and buffeted by what felt like liquid beneath him. His bed was rolling as if it was a ship on the ocean. He looked out into the hallway, and all was normal there: the floor as flat and even as a pane of glass.

He tried to go there.

The walls began to ripple, long streaks from top

to bottom. Then they melted into sheets of rain. The door slammed shut as he approached it in an almost swimming motion. He saw the doorknob melt away and then the door vanished, replaced by a wall of rain. The window was gone, too. The ceiling pulled up and away, revealing a black sky filled with lightning and coal-dark clouds. A crack of booming thunder that he felt in his chest tore over the room, and he began to sink into the floor, drowning—

And then it was gone, all of it.

The room was as it had been, and when he stood up he was as dry as he had been before it started, his sweater neatly pulled into place.

Rain from the storm outside was beating against the window, pushing in at the bottom where he had left it open a crack. He walked to it and slammed the window closed.

Back to normal.

Things are back to normal.

He looked around the room, which looked like it should: bed, rug, wood floor, open suitcase by the door.

And I don't mean this.

The sky cleared at two. As abruptly as the storm had come, it was gone. The house stood dripping water from its eaves around him, a not unpleasant sound. He fixed a late lunch of tuna fish sandwiches, chips, and a couple of beers and took them to the back porch. He watched the sky clear from there.

The air smelled like a colder version of a post-summer storm: fresh but almost icy. The sun popped out of the clouds, and the thousands of raindrops sitting upon the back lawn and unraked leaves suddenly burst into bright sparkles. If the ground was still wet tonight, there would be frost tomorrow morning.

Under the eave of the porch roof, a brilliant rainbow had formed in the sky, and Corrie got up to follow its progress—it arched up and away, and then down again—

It faded away as he watched.

He went back to the ancient Adirondack chair, finished his second beer, and then took the remains of his lunch into the kitchen. There were chucklings and gurglings from the basement, a single loud clang followed by tinkling bells, but he ignored them.

Sun streamed through the windows.

He checked the front porch, but it was too wet to do anything with today.

Perhaps tomorrow . . .

He went upstairs, not looking at the landing or the first step, and went to the guest room next to his bedroom. It, too, had a view out the front of the house, and its window was unimpeded by the large oak tree. He had set up his Nikon with a tele-photo lens on it on a tripod, and aimed it toward the cornfield across Sagett River. With a little positioning, he had been able to focus it on the spot where the scarecrow with the pumpkin's head was stationed.

He looked through the telephoto, but the spot in the cornfield was empty.

He could just make out the pole that the scarecrow had been mounted on.

"I'm not there, I'm here."

Corrie's blood chilled, and he turned away from the camera to see John perched on the end of the guest bed, legs crossed. His head was featureless, and oddly shaped—

John reached up his cornstalk hands and grasped his pumpkin head—with an audible liquid sound he wrenched the pumpkin around 180 degrees. There were carved features on the other side, the ones Corrie remembered—triangle eyes, nose, upwardly sickled mouth with two offset teeth—which now faced Corrie, though the pumpkin was still misshapen.

"Lost my other head I'm afraid, in the service of duty. Picked the first one I found that was the right size," he explained. The smile expanded slightly up at the edges. "What do you think?"

Corrie said nothing.

The smile contracted. "I thought it was time we talk again, Corrie. Today is October fifteenth. You're going to notice things getting much worse the next couple of weeks."

"What do you mean—worse?"

John gave an approximation of a sigh. "Worse."

He held his hands out wide, and looked around him. "You're . . . used to this, more or less. You grew up with it. But it's going to get more . . . intense."

Corrie's already cold blood nearly froze. "I don't think I can handle that."

"All I can tell you is not to worry about it. Things will get very bad later on."

"Later on—"

John held up a hand, and the gesture was almost gentle. "Please. This is as hard for me as it is for you. Harder, perhaps. You may not believe it, but you and I are allies. I've been watching over you for a long time . . ."

"Thanks for nothing."

Again John sighed. "I knew this would be hard, on both of us. All I can tell you now is that when October thirty-first comes, you must be ready. In two weeks . . ."

Corrie waited for him to continue.

"In two weeks, something will happen to you that your whole life since you were very young has been leading up to. It's what all of this"—again he spread his hands—"is for. What it's always been for."

"You mean there's a *reason* for everything I've gone through since I was seven?" In an odd way, Corrie felt almost relief, until John spoke again.

"Oh yes," John said, and his voice, his countenance, became very grim. "There's a reason . . ."

"What is it?" Corrie demanded. "Tell me."

John shook his head. "Not now. But listen to me:

Be careful of that little girl you met today. Watch over her. She's important, too, perhaps more important than you know. And Samhain will try to harm both of you, in whatever way he can—"

As if he had already said too much, John went suddenly quiet.

"I have a thousand questions—"

"I won't answer them," John replied. "Not now. Just believe me that there is an end to all this, and a reason, and that you are an essential part of it. To your world and mine . . ."

"Your world?" His head was spinning with confusion, fear, hope—

John held up a hand. "I've already said too much to you. You must watch Reggie. And soon you will see poor Kathy Marks."

"Kathy Marks . . ."

"These next two weeks, it may seem at times as if you have gone insane—"

Corrie blurted ironic laughter. "And the last twenty-three years?"

The pumpkin face was silent. The features became suddenly frightening, fierce—the mouth straight, the eyes flared with inward light.

John leaned forward, and Corrie was assaulted by a smell unlike any he had ever experienced. It was cold without pity, emptiness itself, the smell of something beyond death.

It was the smell of *nothing*.

"This is what we're dealing with," John said, in a hissing low voice. "I've let a bit of it pass from the

Dark One to this world, to let you see." His hand reached out, impossibly long across the room, and took Corrie's wrist in an iron grip and drew him forward. The arm retreated but brought Corrie to his knees, then closer, and closer still until his face was flat against the pumpkin's own. Corrie's nose nearly snugged into the pumpkin's own nose cavity; his eyes were blinded by the violent light in John's own. Corrie fought against the smell—the *fear*—he felt radiating from John.

The smell got worse, and worse, and now Corrie, on the edge of passing out, felt a terror so horrible and deep that he began to quake and then cry, blurting out, "*No! No, please God, no!*"

He felt his eyes seared, his being violated by something more than filth, more empty and evil than evil itself—

"*That* is what we are dealing with," John said, his voice almost gentle again as he let go of Corrie's wrist. "Something much worse than Samhain. Samhain is only a servant."

Corrie collapsed to the floor, gasping, his face wet with tears.

When he looked up, John was leaning down over him—the light still burned brightly in his eyes, and his mouth was still a straight line.

"*That* is what you and I must fight."

"But—"

"You will see and hear and feel and taste many things that scare you before the end of this," John continued, "but that is what waits at the end."

"Oh, God . . ."

John stood up. He had regained his calmer demeanor; the smile was back on his face, and it widened again at the corners. The fierce, violent light was gone from his eyes.

"Enjoy your dreams, Corrie," John said. He sounded oddly sad and wistful. "They're the only remembrance of your real life that you'll have now."

Chapter Ten

A black and blasted landscape.

The ground underfoot resembled charcoal, of a particularly fine and used-up sort. There were what had been mountains, and a dry, cracked brown riverbed filled with ash. In the far distance a gray-yellow sickly looking haze hovered over the ground, coiling like a snake.

The sky beyond a certain point ended. Sky and earth met in nothingness—as if Columbus had been wrong in this world, and if you sailed too far you would fall from the face of the Earth.

"He has come this far?" the wisp of smoke, which sounded weary of mind and at the same time exhausted physically, said. The wisp of smoke, which ordinarily would hover tall and thin over the ground, was pooled close to the earth, like a fog weighed down by gravity.

His companion, who resembled a more solid

figure but flattened to nearly two dimensions, a kind of cardboard cutout with burning yellow lamps where his eyes would be and a mouth too wide for the face, with just enough depth to give him viability, said in a voice filled with apprehension, "Yes. In two of their weeks there may be nothing left to save."

"Don't say that!" the wisp of smoke shot back angrily; the outburst seemed to weaken him further, the cloud that contained him sinking ever lower to the ground.

"The girl—" the cardboard man began.

"The girl is only our backup plan," the wisp of smoke said. It was measuring its words now, speaking slowly, almost whispering. As it did so it began to elongate a bit. "She was to be used in case there was a standoff. But now . . ." It added after a moment, "I don't know if the young man is capable."

The wisp of smoke was quiet, watching the roiling sickly fog in the distance, the ruined, blackened rolling hills, the emptiness at the horizon.

"The Dark One may win—" the cardboard cutout said.

"No! That can never happen. It would be the end of everything. For all of us."

"But we knew he would try this in the end."

"Yes. I think even he knew his other attempts, through Samhain, would fail. It was more of a game to him. He would have taken the easy way if it had worked. But now . . ." The wisp of smoke gave his version of a grim smile. "Now he's taken the hard way. And the girl cannot be readied later. We will have to prepare her now, so that she can be used if necessary."

"But she is so young—"

"It can't be helped. We have no choice. I . . . feel sorry for her. For them both. But it's for them as well as us . . ."

"I understand," the wisp of smoke's companion said. "We will do what has to be done."

"All of us," the wisp of smoke said. Again he gave a grim smile, watching the edge of the world grow emptier before his eyes. The cardboard cutout moved silently away, leaving him to his own thoughts.

"All of us . . ." he repeated, sighing.

Chapter Eleven

"Gina, it's time for bed!"

Marcia Bright could hear her daughter playing in her room, even though she had tucked Gina into bed a half hour before. The child never stopped. She was what Marcia called an Energy Vampire—she sucked the energy out of any room, and humans that were in it, and used it all in her little dynamo way. She never stopped. From seven in the morning when she got up to go to school, to ten at night when she finally went to bed, she never stopped.

"Ginaaaaa!"

There was no answer from upstairs—but still Marcia could hear her daughter talking and laughing—

"I'm gonna kill that kid—" she said wearily, getting up from the family room couch with a groan and putting her slippers on. Beside her, half asleep in front of the sitcom rerun they were watching or tv, Ted grunted and said, "Want me to go?"

Marcia watched him close his eyes as the words left his lips. "I wish," she said, under her breath.

She walked three steps and then turned around seeing him open his eyes again and reach for the popcorn they'd made.

"You faking bastard," she said.

Ted laughed. "I'll leave you some popcorn," he said, remoting the channel to a basketball game.

"Jeez . . ."

Marcia shuffled in her slippers to the stairs, and then up them.

She was surprised to see no light beneath Gina's door. But, from experience, she knew that mean nothing. There was probably a flashlight missing from the kitchen junk drawer, and Gina would be under the covers with a book, or a stack of Legos building a castle or tearing it down . . .

There was still plenty of noise issuing from the room—grunts and yelps and hoots of laughter.

"Ginaaaa!"

The sounds continued.

She eased open Gina's bedroom door, and wa again surprised—no glow from beneath the covers

"Did you just switch that flashlight off—?"

The noises continued in the darkness.

"Young lady—" Marcia began, switching on the room light.

It flared on overhead—showing her daughte peacefully asleep in bed.

"Wha—"

Marcia walked purposefully over to the bed and looked down. Gina looked asleep, her head denting her pillow, her thumb planted just at her lips, her rag doll nested nearby.

"If you're faking like your father—"

She reached down to shake her daughter, then hesitated.

Gina looked so peacefully asleep.

Marcia retreated to the doorway, flipped off the light, frowning.

The noises immediately started again in the room—hoots, whistles, a clang like a fire bell . . .

Marcia had a quick intake of breath; she flipped the light switch on—

The sounds vanished.

Switch off: a ripping sound, hissing laughter that faded into a basso chuckling voice—

"*Ted!*"

The urgency in her voice brought her husband bounding up the stairs. It also awoke Gina, who sat up in bed, rubbing her eyes.

The noises were gone.

Marcia flipped the switch on and off, then on again, but nothing happened.

"What is it?" Ted said, reaching the doorway. He looked into the room. "Was she asleep?"

Gina yawned and looked at them. "Time for school do I need to get up is the sun up—?"

"No, baby. Go back to sleep. I'll wake you up when it's time."

"I was dreamin' about the time we went to Disney World just like we were there again nothing strange like in dreams and Dad was yelling on the water ride just like he did—"

"Hush," Marcia said, putting her finger to her lips. "Go back to sleep. Back to Disney World."

"What's wrong?" Ted said.

"I . . . nothing, I guess," his wife answered. Gina lay back down in bed. Marcia's fingers hesitated on the light switch, then flipped it off. The room went dark and silent.

"What the hell—" Ted began.

"Sorry," Marcia said. "Thought I heard some noises in the room. It's all right."

"But—"

"Let's go finish the popcorn."

She took his arm, and steered him downstairs.

Later that night, much later, in the quiet dark time before the world rolls toward dawn, Marcia Bright sat up in her own bed, with her husband gently snoring beside her, and heard from her daughter's room across the hall what sounded like the whistling of a teakettle, the snapping of many fingers, a chorus of ghostly singing voices . . .

Chapter Twelve

Jerry Farrow had never, as far as Grant knew, been a happy man. He had spent his entire career in the police department clawing his way to the top. From the moment he had hit the pavement as a beat cop, that one goal—to be captain—had possessed and overwhelmed him. Grant had never heard him speak about his family, his vacations, his hobbies; never heard him talk about sports, or women, or even the crazy things that happened on the job. When he drove a cruiser, his partners, who didn't stay that way long, disliked him with a passion. When he was promoted from uniform to detective, just after Grant, he looked at Grant as a rival, not a colleague, and treated him as such. When Grant called him on it, he never forgot. And when he finally made captain, he made sure to remember.

Captain Farrow sat behind his desk with his perpetual scowl on his face—he held up a file and shook it in Grant's direction.

"Something tells me you were looking at this," Farrow nearly spit. His close-set, small dark eyes tried to bore into Grant, who merely stared over the top of Farrow's balding head.

"And that would be—" Grant began mildly.

Farrow let the file drop onto his desk. "Corrie Phaeder. You know damn well he's back in Orangefield. I want you to leave him alone."

"Why wouldn't I?"

Farrow made a noise in his throat that sounded like a spit. "Don't go anywhere near him. If you do I'll suspend you so fast your ass will pucker."

"Is that all?"

Farrow tried to measure him with his eyes, but Grant continued to stare blithely over his head.

"Get out of my office."

Grant turned to leave, thinking, *What I do on my own time has nothing to do with you, bastard.*

The drive out to Riley Gates's farm was a pleasant one. It was one of those perfect autumn days in upstate New York, cool yet mild, sun bright, with a sky as deep and clear as blue ice. Grant had the window down in the car, and the radio on, and examined the farms to either side of the road—it seemed like every square inch of Orangefield was overgrown with pumpkins. The hillsides were so bright orange it hurt his eyes. The fields were one huge blanket the color of Halloween.

The farms looked so much alike that he drove right by Gates's, then immediately braked when he passed a sign that read *Riley's Pick Your Own Pumpkins*. He backed up and there was the rutted road that led to Gates's place. He carefully drove his Taurus through untended potholes toward the distant farm house and barn. It was all out of a picture book: white clapboard house, faded red barn, the fields full of pumpkins.

And Riley had been the best cop he ever met.

His friend, looking like any other stout farmer in bib overalls and faded baseball cap, was waiting for him in front of the house. Grant parked the car by the open barn and got out.

"When the hell you gonna fix that drive of yours?" Grant complained.

Gates laughed. "Never. Keeps the riffraff out." As Grant ambled up to him he put out his hand. "How the hell are ya, podner?"

Grant took the large, rough paw in his own. "Passable."

"Bullshit. You've got that look in your eyes." Gates took his hand back and turned toward the house. "Come and have a little lunch. We'll talk."

"You're not gonna drag me up to the attic to look at your model trains?"

Gates laughed. "Not right now. Got a new diesel engine I want to show you, but we'll save it for next time. Other stuff we need to talk about today."

Grant followed Riley to the back of the farmhouse, where a meal was waiting on a table covered with a red and white checkered cloth flanked by two white wicker chairs, set back out of the sun under an overhang of the house that formed a natural patio covering. A basket of chicken was flanked by a bowl of potato salad and a plate filled with ears of corn. Next to the table was an open cooler filled with iced beer.

Grant put his hand into the cooler, savoring the chill of the melting ice; he looked at Riley. "You?"

"None for me," Riley said, sighing. "Diabetes says no. I sneak one every once in a while, but I pay for it." He patted his stomach as he sat down with a grunt. "Feet hurt all the time, when they don't go numb on me. I should lose the weight, but then I wouldn't feel like me." He turned his piercing stare on Grant as he sat down. "So how's Jerry Farrow?"

Grant twisted the cap off his bottle of beer and took a swallow. "Same as ever. Grade-A asshole."

Riley grunted a laugh. "Was a fine day when I retired, just to avoid that prick." He loaded his plate with a single small chicken drumstick, a half ear of corn, a spoonful of potato salad. "And how's Rose?"

Grant, in the middle of filling his own plate with considerably more food than his host, furrowed his brow. "Not so good, Riley. I may have to put her in Killborne again."

"I'm sorry to hear that."

"She's getting worse. And no matter what her doctors seem to do with her medication, it doesn't work for long. When the side effects start she stops taking it altogether, and then . . ." He shrugged.

"God, she was a wonderful lady, though."

Grant picked up the past tense, and didn't dispute it. Riley had never been one to dance around anything. "Yes, she surely was. About the most wonderful woman I ever met."

Grant nodded his assent.

Gates went on, "I can't imagine how hard it must be to see someone you love change into . . . something else."

"It happened to her mother, too. We should have seen it coming—"

Riley waved a hand in impatience. "Pah. The reason's irrelevant. It happened, and you've got to deal with it. Just like I had to deal with Dierdre leaving me." He laughed. "The witch."

Grant laughed, too. The mood had lightened. He pointed to the chicken and was about to speak when Riley cut him off.

"The bucket's inside. They deliver now. You didn't think I *cooked* this stuff, did you?"

Grant howled and reached into the cooler for another beer. For a moment he was at peace, the day perfect, sun warm on his back, sky deep blue from horizon to horizon, having lunch with his closest friend and mentor . . .

"What's troubling you, Billy boy?" Riley said in a soft voice. He was sitting back, regarding Grant with an almost magisterial look. He would have made a good judge.

Grant sighed. "Weird shit."

Gates's face broke into a wide grin. "Ha! I had an inkling we'd be having this conversation some day. You always were too hard-headed for the soft sciences." He leaned his bulk forward, resting his forearms on the table. His eyes squinted in concentration. "Let me tell you something about yourself, boyo."

"Uh-oh," Grant said. "Lecture mode."

Gates nodded once, briskly. "I happen to know a thing or two about you, that you're not aware of yourself. I was born here in Orangefield. I know you always thought that was a disadvantage to you, but it wasn't. Gave you a perspective us natives didn't always have. But, on the flip side, it made you crazy when you came up against some of our little burg's . . . peculiarities, shall we say."

"Weird shit."

Riley hooted laughter. "Exactly. You didn't know how to handle it back then, and you don't know how to handle it now."

"Well, how *do* you handle it?" Grant briefly told his friend about his visit to Fred Willims's home, what he had found there, and what had happened to the bee keeper.

Riley sat back and whistled. "That's a good one, I'll admit. A real good one. You noticed that the *Herald* only said suicide was suspected. Now *they* know how to handle a story." He couldn't keep the irony out of his voice.

"Anything to protect the tourist industry," Grant huffed. "But you and me—"

"I'll tell you how I handled it, always," Gates said. "I officially ignored the hell out of it."

"But—"

Gates held up a hand. "Let me finish. As far as police work went, I did my job, as you know, and did it damned well if I say so. But let's just say I kept two sets of files. One for the police department, and," he tapped his baseball cap, "one in here. And then, on long winter nights, when the cold winds were blowing and when I wasn't missing my Dierdre, the witch, I'd take out my second set of files and look them over."

"You never talked with me about this," Grant said.

Gates smiled thinly. "Never talked with *anybody* about it, boyo. Nothing but trouble to do so. And they're *my* files. You've got to make your own."

Grant said, "They're growing thick, the last year or so."

Riley nodded. "I thought as much. You've got the look, the hard head getting a little soft. My advice, and it's free, is to do as I did, and keep those two file systems separate." He looked first at one index finger, then the other. "Police shit over here, weird shit over here. Now regarding Corrie Phaeder, for instance . . ."

"You old goat!" Grant said, stunned.

Riley smiled enigmatically. "I knew that's why

93

you came out here to see your old friend. Little birdies still talk to me, or I talk to them. I knew the Phaeder boy had come home to roost, just as I knew that you wouldn't be able to stay away from him. It was, if I recall, Jerry Farrow's single biggest fuck-up, was it not?"

Grant sat silent, and nodded.

"Sure it was. I would imagine that by this time you've been to see the boy, at least once. And I imagine you looked through the old file, and Farrow has given you a warning, which you have no intention of heeding." Gates made a steeple of his fingers, and looked over it. "Am I warm?"

"Very."

"Good. And my advice. . . ." Gates suddenly leaned forward, and made a gimme motion at the cooler. "Let me have one of those cold ones, Billy boy. I'll pay for it later, but I don't care."

Grant dutifully uncapped a beer bottle and handed it to him.

Riley made a great show of drinking the beer, and put it down, half finished, on the table. "Listen close now, because pretty soon all these beautiful pumpkins around us will be picked, and I'll be spending all my time out on my little farm making a buck or two." He finished the beer, belched, and put his hands on the table. His eyes became hard as marbles. "Two things here. One: that Phaeder kid did not, I repeat, did *not* kill his mother. And two: someone else did."

"Wha—"

"Let me finish. Unbeknownst to you or Farrow or anyone else, I made a little file of my own on this one." He tapped his head. "Let's just say it bothered me the way it was handled by the department, and the reaming out you took on it. I even tried to talk to the kid, but he was gone by then. I did get the real estate agent, that bitch Lucy Williams, to let me have a look around the house. And my own conclusion is that everyone, including you, bungled that one."

Again Grant tried to interrupt, but was kept at bay.

"Look at where she was found, Bill. The crime scene photographs. She had multiple stab wounds. The boy was confined to a wheelchair upstairs. For him to kill her he would have had to stab her at the top of the stairs. Yes, she was found at the bottom of the stairs, on the landing. But her neck wasn't broken. There was barely a mark on her, Bill."

For emphasis he picked up the cleaned drumstick on his plate and snapped it in half.

"There was someone else in that house. Someone very good, who didn't leave a fingerprint or a mark of his presence."

Riley's eyes were even harder. "Correct. Which means . . . ?"

He savagely tapped his head. "Farrow botched it, because he refused to consider that anyone other than Corrie Phaeder killed his mother. And you botched it even worse, because you wouldn't look at it as what you call 'weird shit.' Farrow's a moron, but you're not, so you have no excuse. And it's some of the weirdest shit this town has seen yet." He gave a great sigh. "And I have a very bad feeling about it."

"Then who," Grant said with emphasis, "killed Corrie Phaeder's mother?"

Riley took his baseball cap off, scratched his head, put the baseball cap back on. He looked out over the pumpkin fields.

"I miss that Aaron Peters," he said. "Remember him? Kid they used to call The Pumpkin Tender?"

"You're avoiding my question? All right, I'll play along. I remember him. Blew his brains out last year."

"Yup. Suicide, plain and clear. Good kid. Got messed up in the Army in Somalia. He told me a few things one day when he was here, looking after my fields. I sat him down where you're sitting, and after a couple of beers he started to talk. The name Samhain came up."

"You mean that Lord of Death crap?"

Riley looked at the sky, the horizon. "Yup. That Kerlan fellow, case you had with that bee keeper Willims involved, the name came up there, too, didn't it?"

"He wrote a children's book—"

"*Sam Hain and the Halloween that Almost Wasn't.* I've got a copy somewhere in the house. Cute book." He tapped his head. "Big file in here with the name Samhain on it. Very big."

He gave Grant his hardest look yet. "In fact,

over the years, seems like all my other files sooner or later end up in that one big one. Something I'd look into if I was you. You could start with a family named Reynolds. The father's dead, but the wife and son live in Orangefield." He smiled like the Cheshire cat. "You'll like the son. He knows just about everything there is to know about Samhain."

Grant studied his friend carefully. "You're not pulling my leg about any of this?"

Riley's smile turned into a glare. "You asked me who killed Corrie Phaeder's mother. Well . . . I think it's pretty clear, ain't it?"

Grant stared at him as if he had gone mad. Riley made a motion at the cooler again.

"Gimme another one."

Grant did as he was told. As he passed the cold bottle into his friend's hand he said, "You're telling me this weird shit really is . . . *weird* shit?"

"Have I ever lied to you, Billy boy?"

"No."

"Something very screwy has been going on in this town, and for quite some time. And now I think it's coming to some sort of a head." Gates studied his beer. When he spoke again his voice was lower, ruminative. "Remember what happened that day with Kathy Marks and Corrie Phaeder?"

Grant was silent.

"I would have shot you, you know. If you hadn't put down your gun when I told you to, I would have shot you dead to save that boy."

"I believe you."

"Then believe me when I say this. Every ounce of cop sense I've ever had tells me that we are in for a bumpy ride in Orangefield. And I want you to be ready for it. And whatever else you believe, believe this: Corrie Phaeder didn't kill his own mother. You'll have a lot less trouble if you get your head around that."

Riley Gates looked at his friend, and suddenly smiled. His beer bottle was empty.

"Hand me another one, would you, Billy boy?"

Chapter Thirteen

Dreaming reality again.

This was exactly as it happened: His mother came up with his lunch tray at exactly twelve-thirty. She was always very punctual. He could hear the television set downstairs, turned very loud because she refused to wear her hearing-aid because it made her 'look crippled.' Fifty-eight years old and still as vain as when she was twenty. It was one of the game shows, The Price Is Right, *and after that would come three endless hours of soap operas: As the World Turns, General Hospital . . .*

She put the tray down on his lap as he sat in the wheelchair and backed away.

"Can you close the door when you leave?" he said, testily.

She cringed at the harshness in his voice; he wanted to yell at her, "Don't cower!" and at the same time he wanted her to hold him like he was a baby.

"The noises—" she said.

"I can't do anything about the noises, dammit!" *he shouted at her, and she almost dropped the tray and ran out of the room.*

That's my mother, *he thought.* That frightened, twitchy, saucer-eyed skinny hag is the woman who brought me into the world, and is supposed to protect me. But she's more frightened than I am. And now maybe I *can* do something about the noises, and the rest of it.

He grabbed a corner of the quilt covering his lap and twisted it, angrily. He was suddenly ashamed.

"I'm sorry—!" he shouted through the door, which she had left open—but she was too far away to hear. The television had been turned up even louder, and he could hear her banging around down there, in the kitchen, making her own lunch.

Suddenly the room around him twisted out of shape, as if it was made of soft taffy and some giant had taken hold of it. The walls squeezed sideways, the baseball posters on them turning 180 degrees and contracting to long thin lines. The closet disappeared into the bubbling distorted wall and the window was snuffed out, making the room dark. A rhythmic thumping noise from somewhere above, undercut by a skreeee skreeee sound became louder and louder until he had to cover his ears.

He closed his eyes.

The sounds stopped.

He opened his eyes, and the room was as it had been. He looked at the lunch on his bed tray—the in-

evitable tuna fish sandwich, cup of lemon tea and an apple. He picked up one half of the sandwich (cut diagonally, of course, the crusts removed) and as he brought it up to his lips the tuna salad within turned to something resembling sawdust and trickled out of the edges of the bread. As the sawdust bits hit the tray they turned into red ants, which scurried all over the tray, covering the apple, climbing into the tea cup, frantically swimming.

He dropped the sandwich half, and as it hit the plate it turned into a tuna salad sandwich again, and the ants disappeared.

He closed his eyes, jammed the same half sandwich into his mouth, and felt tuna salad turn into crawling ants as he took the first bite.

He gagged the sandwich out onto the plate. Disgustedly, he picked up the tray and put it on the nearby bed.

The room twisted sideways again, and then came back to normal with a twang *sound.*

From downstairs, he heard his mother cry out.

"Mother!" *he called, at first peevishly and then, when her cry of pain was repeated, with alarm.*

"Mother, what's wrong!"

Leave Orangefield, *the voice in his head said.*

"How did you—"

I know, *the voice said.* If you stay I'll kill her. Talk to her, she knows now, too.

His mother appeared in the doorway, eyes wide with fright.

"You're going to leave me," she gasped.

"I—"

101

"Don't deny it! The one thing I ever asked of you is that you don't leave me alone. I've given you everything, done everything for you since you were a baby. Your father left me, and now you're going to leave me too—"

"Mother—"

"I can see it in your eyes! If you stay this house will leave us alone! I know it!"

"If I stay this house will destroy me. It's wanted to kill me since I was seven years old."

"That's not true! It's just noises—"

"It's not just noises! For you it's just noises! How many times do I have to tell you? The only time things are real to me is when I sleep! When I wake up the world turns into a nightmare for me!"

As if on cue, the room canted again, his mother in the doorway suddenly horizontal and stretched out to twenty foot length. Then everything was normal again, though the floor now had valleys and mountains in it, and his mother looked as if she were a mile away, tiny at the top of a peak which filled the doorway.

"You're my son!" she pleaded, her voice a distant echo, and then she was there again, full size.

Corrie said, "I can't live like this any more, Mother. I bought a ticket two days ago, over the phone. A cab is picking me up tomorrow morning. The airlines will have a wheelchair for me, so I'll leave this one here. Things will be better after I'm gone. The noises will stop."

She ran forward and knelt in front of him. "You can't leave me alone!"

"If I don't leave this house will kill me."

"You have to take care of me!"

He turned the wheelchair away from her. "Go watch your shows," *he said.*

She moaned, and he heard her crying and then finally he heard her get up and leave the room.

He turned the wheelchair around and faced the door.

An unearthly scream filled the house. The television went impossibly loud, then silent.

Corrie moved the wheelchair to the doorway, then bumped it over the sill out into the hallway.

"Mother?"

He heard a rhythmic thumping sound coming from downstairs.

He rolled the wheelchair to the top of the stairs.

"Mother—?"

The word caught in his throat. At the bottom of the stairs, his mother lay bleeding. Dead. The front door was wide open.

"What are you doing!" *Corrie screamed overhead.* "You can't do this!"

Actually, I can do whatever I want.

"I'll go—"

Too late, *the voice said.* Go to California.

"You k—"

Yes. And I'll kill you, too, if you come back.

And then it laughed.

Chapter Fourteen

"Hey Mom! The playmates want somethin' to eat! Can they have something to eat can they can they?"

Down in the kitchen, with the ironing board out and the nine inch television showing the opening credits of *Days of Our Lives*, Marcia Bright groaned.

"Tell 'em to come down and get it themselves!"

"Awww, Mom!"

Marcia turned her attention back to the television.

In the back of her mind, something *pinged*, but she stored it away for later.

Twenty minutes into the soap opera, Gina appeared in the kitchen, frowning.

"They went away," she said, frowning. "They said maybe they'd be back later but for now they

Al Sarrantonio

have somewhere else to go but they'll be back they said."

Marcia turned away from the television, where a commercial for fabric softeners was showing, and gave her daughter part of her attention.

"How many times have I told you not to run your sentences together, Gina? Do you want to end up in speech therapy class in school?"

Gina turned away and shrugged. "Whatever you say, Mom." Marcia had to laugh as Gina was consciously trying to stop talking. It didn't work.

Gina turned around and put her hands on her hips. "But if you'd fed the playmates they wouldn't have left and then I wouldn't be alone now and bothering you and—"

That little *ping* sounded again in the back of Marcia's mind, and she gave all her attention to her daughter, even though the soap was back on. She turned down the volume on the television set.

"Gina, remember a few nights ago, when you were having a dream about Disney World, and then you woke up and there was all kinds of sounds in your room?"

Gina eyed her carefully, as if weighing what to say.

"Sure. . . ."

Marcia tried to sound casual, but knew it didn't work. "Has that happened again?"

"What do you mean?" Her daughter was still measuring her words, which was always a sure sign

106

that she was trying to hide something—otherwise everything would come out in a rush.

Marcia knelt down and put her hands gently on her daughter's shoulders, staring at her.

Gina tried to look away.

"Gina, look at me," her mother soothed. "Good. Now, answer this question. Have any of the noises from the other night come back?"

A light flared in her daughter's eyes. "No, Mom. Can I go now?"

"No you can't. Have you heard any other kind of noises since that night?"

Gina stiffened. "Well . . ."

"What were they?" Marcia let a dram of parental authority replace her friendly tone.

Gina looked away, up at the ceiling, then said. "Just other stuff. Waterfalls, and a fire engine bell."

"When?"

Gina shrugged. "Whenever they want."

"Who's 'they,' Gina?"

Her daughter tried to squirm out of her grip. "Let me go and play!"

"Not until you tell me who 'they' is."

"Nobody! There's nobody and now you're hurting me let me go!"

Gina twisted out of her grip and ran upstairs.

Marcia, still kneeling on the floor, realized that she *had* been gripping her daughter too tight. She looked at her hands, and slowly rose. After a moment's contemplation, she turned back to the television and her kitchen chores. She turned the television back up, but not too loud, and kept half an ear cocked toward the upstairs.

When the playmates came back, Gina read them the riot act: don't be loud, and don't leave again until she told them to.

With hoots and whistles, they agreed.

"And no more big tricks, like moving the walls around you hear me?" she scolded, and again the amorphous forms, which looked something like see-through children, nodded.

Though she had enjoyed the window being on the opposite wall, and letting her look straight into the bathroom next door.

They played quietly for a while, the playmates making hissing noises when they were annoyed and little doglike yelps when they were content. Gina had laid out a tea party on the floor, with all four of her cups and saucers for the playmates and an empty Play-doh can for her own cup. She served plastic carrots and yellow construction paper cutouts, which she told them was corn. They played along, just as they always did.

In the few days since the playmates had come, she had been able to tell the difference between the four of them, and given them names. There was Andy, the tallest one, who she had decided to marry when they were both grown up. There were the twins (they weren't exactly alike, but enough so

that she had decided they were twins) Harry and
Mary, who were slight and sometimes faded out altogether. And then there was Judith, by far the
most substantial, who looked almost real except
for her animal legs (they looked like a donkey's
legs) and holes where her eyes should be. She
could be the meanest, not only to Gina but to the
other three playmates, and she was the one who
usually told them to leave. Sometimes she didn't
act like a kid at all.

"Are you their mother?" Gina asked her, as the
thought suddenly occurred to her.

There were hoots and hisses from all four, and
Andy bent over double, as if he was laughing.

"Guess not," Gina said, "because if you were
their mother they couldn't laugh at you without
being punished which is what my mother does all
the time do you have mothers where you come
from?"

Again the hissing and hooting.

Gina sipped at her imaginary tea, and ordered
the other four to do so. So far they hadn't been
able to directly touch anything, but Judith had
managed to knock over Gina's pyramid of stuffed
animals as she walked through it.

"What's it like in your world is it like this with
trees and a river and clouds and ants that get into
the kitchen?"

She waited for an answer, but there was none;
the four playmates just stared at her (or something
like it) and then the room got very bright and she

felt a ripple beneath her as if someone had taken the rug in hand and given it a *snap* to put runs in it. One wall got very long like a tunnel and turned dark as midnight and then with a loud click like a camera shutter was back to the way it had been.

"You sure can do a lot of tricks in your world do you like magic?"

The four of them, who were now fading and then becoming more distinct, just stared at her.

"Drink your tea don't you like it I made it just for you!"

She picked up her empty Play-doh can, which still smelled of that wonderful clay, and feigned sipping.

The hoots and whistles increased in volume, and the floor began to spin slowly around, taking her with it, as if she was on a giant top.

"Hey! Mom's gonna hear be quiet!"

The floor spun faster, and Gina snugged both hands down into the shag rug, gripping tight. It was fun, but she was starting to get dizzy. The walls, the window, the pictures over her bed were melting into a kind of buttery color.

"I said stop!"

The floor came to an abrupt stop amidst a loud bass drum sound. The four playmates were fading.

"Where are you going stay with me don't go!"

Judith said something that wasn't a hoot or whistle but words, and then they were gone.

Gina still felt as if she was spinning, and stood

up, laughing slightly as she stepped forward but went sideways.

She took another wobbly step and fell down—

—into her mother's embrace in the doorway, where she stood with a frozen look of terror on her face.

"Gina—"

"They're gone Mom the playmates are gone but they'll be back later they had to go over to Mr. Phaeder's house I met him last week sorry he seems like a nice man sorry."

Chapter Fifteen

As he pried open the third can of new paint, Corrie watched, out of the corner of his eye, the car parked down the road. It had been there for nearly an hour with a single occupant in the driver's seat. The driver hadn't made a move to drive away or get out of the car.

Corrie went back to work, laying the lid on the spread newspapers under the paint can and giving the paint a vigorous stirring with the wooden mixer Sears had provided.

When he turned around with his paint brush in hand, someone was standing right in front of him.

"Jeez—" he exclaimed, his breath catching in his throat.

He stood up to face his visitor.

It was Kathy Marks.

"*Jeez!*" Corrie repeated, with different emphasis. The librarian gave a weak, tentative smile.

"Sorry I snuck up on you like that. I've spent the last hour trying to work up the courage to get out of my car."

"I would have come to see you eventually . . ."

She studied his face, his eyes. "I believe you would have. It would have been a braver thing than me coming here."

He gave his own tentative smile. "I would have visited you at the library, Kathy."

She nodded. "I moved out of the house a long time ago. I live in an apartment now."

"I hope the house burned down."

Silence hung in the air between them at his sudden blurt of truth.

Corrie, as if snapping out of a trance, suddenly breathed deeply and put down his paintbrush. He checked his hands to see if they were soiled with paint, wiped them on his pants to be sure, and stuck out his hand. A genuine smile had replaced his experimental one.

"I'm glad to see you, Kathy."

Her warm hand slipped into his, gripped lightly and let go. She nodded, her eyes never leaving his. "It's good to see you, too, Corrie."

Ten minutes later found them side by side in rockers on the finished part of the porch. Corrie had made lemonade and, to his surprise, Kathy Mark had followed him into the house and helped. A few low sounds—snorts and something that sounded like a shovel being dragged across gravel, came from the basement and second floor, but Corrie ignored them.

"Still have your companions?" Kathy remarked.

"Yes," Corrie said simply, handing her the finished pitcher of lemonade, while he handled the two tall glasses.

On the porch, Kathy rocked gently for a while, studying the rushing river across the street. "I never realized how beautiful it is over here," she finally said.

"It was a boy's dream—until I hit seven years old."

She turned in her chair to regard him. "You met me when you were nine."

"And you were twelve. That's not what I meant."

"Didn't you?"

"Well . . . that became another kind of boy's dream . . ."

"And nightmare." Her laugh was hollow, tired.

"Look, Kathy—"

"Maybe it was a mistake to come here. A big one." She put her lemonade down and stared at him, unblinking. "But when I heard you were back I knew I had to see you."

Corrie was about to answer when she went on, looking out at the river again, rocking herself gently. "I never got over you, you know. For the last twelve years, whenever a relationship petered out after a few dates, I blamed it on you. But I wasn't really being honest with myself. I should have blamed it on me."

She stopped rocking and looked at him again. "The only thing you did wrong was not telling me you were leaving. I know how it must have been with your mother dying, but to pick up and leave like that, as soon as you got the all-clear, without telling me . . ."

"If I had told you, I wouldn't have been able to leave."

"Is it that simple?"

He gave a slight, wry smile. "Nothing between us was ever simple."

She regarded the river again. "That's true. In a lot of ways, it was a sick relationship."

"Kathy—"

"No, let me finish. I've had twelve years to think about it. You know I didn't have the courage to talk about it then—you told me so yourself. But it isn't courage now, either. It's just that I'm tired. Tired of everything . . ."

She closed her eyes, kept rocking gently.

"Do you know I almost did it again last Halloween? There were two more suicides, and a little girl named Annabeth Turner was supposed to be the third. She was eleven, just like I was that first time. And then that *thing* in my head came back. And when Annabeth wouldn't go through with it I found myself standing on a chair with a rope around my neck again." She looked at him blankly. "And this time I wanted to."

Corrie was staring at her wide-eyed.

She nodded sadly, her head resting against the

chair cushion. "I wanted to for a lot of reasons. You were only one of them. My . . . life was one of them. But most of all"—a strange light came into her eyes—"I wanted to because this time *I saw something.* That voice promised me I'd see my mother and father, and this time *something was there.*"

"Your parents?" Corrie said in awe.

Still resting her head back on the cushion, she turned to smile at him and shook her head. "No. But *something* was there. I know it."

"But—"

She shook her head more vigorously, closing her eyes. "No 'buts,' Corrie. I told you I've had a lot of time to think. I've done a lot of it since that day last Halloween. There was something there, something after this world, and I caught a glimpse of it. It was real. And no one's going to tell me otherwise."

"But what if it was just an illusion, like the things in my room—"

"Ha!" It was a weak laugh. Her eyes were open again, and boring into him. "You think those are illusions? Do you know why I bonded with you so closely when we met? Because you were going through the same kind of thing. I thought you had part of the answer. I wanted so badly to know why I had been picked, why I had almost let it happen. It was only later, when you were sixteen and I was nineteen . . ."

A touch of color came to her cheeks.

"I did love you," Corrie said.

117

"And I loved you, more than you can imagine. When you left, it was like having part of my flesh ripped away."

"I had to go. If I hadn't, this house would have killed me."

"But you came back."

"Yes. And now I'm sure it's going to kill me."

"You could have taken me with you!" Sudden tears formed. She covered her eyes with her hands. Then she was sobbing. "You could have taken me with you and we could have fought it together . . ."

Corrie said nothing, and then he said, "If I had taken you it would have started all over again, in California. All the . . . problems we had."

She turned on him fiercely. "You don't know that!"

"I do. Don't you remember the last time we were together, Kathy? With Detective Grant aiming a handgun at me?"

She pushed with her hands, as if warding off something. *"Yes! Yes! I remember!* Oh, God . . ."

"Can you tell me if we'd gone to California together that wouldn't have happened again, and again, until finally we did it?"

She got up, knocked her lemonade glass over, sobbed and moved blindly toward the porch steps. "Oh, God, I should never have come here, never . . ."

Corrie stared at the pool of spilled lemonade, the broken shards of glass; one of them formed a

118

tiny prism, breaking light into the colors of the rainbow.

"Kathy . . ." he said half-heartedly as she reached the bottom of the steps, and stood heaving sobs into her hands.

He got up and went to her, hesitated, then put his arms around her.

"Kathy . . ." he whispered.

She pulled away, then suddenly turned in to him. "Oh, Corrie, why couldn't we have made something out of it . . ."

"We did," he whispered. "But it was something destructive. It was destroying both of us. That's why I went away. To save me—and to save you, too."

She held him tighter. "I just wanted to die. I just wanted . . ."

"I know," he said. Then he added, "I didn't."

After a moment she snuffled a halting, ironic laugh and pulled away from him enough to show him a halting smile. Her face was streaked with tears, her eyes puffy.

"Want to hear something funny?" she said. The smile wavered. "Do you know who saved me when I was hanging from that oak tree last Halloween? It was Annabeth Turner, the eleven-year-old. She cut me down. She had the *thing* in her head, too, and she fought it off and cut me down. And I went there to save *her* . . ."

Sobbing again, she pushed away from Corrie and

went quickly to her car. She opened the door, and before she got in she turned to look back at him.

"There *is* something there," she said, and then she climbed quickly into the car and started it up, turned it around and drove away.

Corrie stared after her, then stood watching the spot where her car had been; then he remounted the steps and cleaned up the spilled lemonade and broken glass with one of his paint rags. He retrieved his paint brush and was about to resume work on the unpainted part of the porch when he heard another sound behind him.

He turned, expecting to find Kathy Marks returned, but it was a trim short woman in jeans and a tee-shirt that said, I SURVIVED MONDAY! She had short black hair in a cut that looked familiar.

Corrie had no doubt that she also had a similar tee-shirt for every other day of the week.

The woman stopped about five feet up the walk and shaded her eyes with her right hand. "Are you Corrie Phaeder?" she asked, in a demanding tone.

"Yes, I am. And you—"

"Stay the hell away from my daughter!" the woman said. The shading hand dropped into a fist from which an accusing index finger jabbed at him.

"I—"

She pointed to her left without letting him speak. "I'm Marcia Bright, Gina's mother."

"You mean Reggie?"

"Her name isn't Reggie! It's Gina!" She was trembling with anger or perhaps fear.

He took a step off the porch, and she backed up one step. "Stay the hell away from her! And me!"

"Mrs. Bright, I'm sorry, but Gina wandered over here one day while I was working outside and talked to me for a few minutes—"

"And then the trouble started! As soon as she came over to this . . ."—she jabbed angrily at the house—"goddamned haunted house, it all started!"

Corrie held his spread hands out. "I have no idea—"

"If you go near her again I'll call the police! I've already called them! I don't give a damn what you do in your own home, but leave mine alone! Now she has playmates, and sees all kinds of things in her room—"

Oh, God.

Corrie thought of what John had told him.

Oh, God, it's starting for her.

"Mrs. Bright, please—"

"My husband has a gun, and I know how to use it—*stay away from all of us!*"

She turned and stumbled away, her steps turning into a halting run.

Corrie stared after her.

The day, which had darkened, turned suddenly darker.

From within the house, he heard a chorus of loud bangs, and scrapes, and a whoosh like the close passing of a freight train.

Oh, God. Her too . . .

Chapter Sixteen

The Pumpkin Festival came to Orangefield.

Most of the pumpkins were picked, the fields growing bare, turning from bright orange to muddy brown. The orange ring around Orangefield contracted into the town itself, pumpkins everywhere, making it bright as the sun. Deformed Halloween fruit, kicked in by careless pickers or grown too grotesque to sell, sat in place, alone, forgotten. The cut vines withered from green to gray, became part of the soil from which they sprang.

The days became colder, the nights were crisp as cider.

The town of Orangefield went from bland to blinding. The color orange was everywhere. An orange stripe marking the coming parade route was painted down the middle of Main Street. Store fronts were filled with pumpkin goods and pumpkin cutouts, making them orange windows. Plywood painted pumpkins, four feet in width, were hoisted under every street light along the route where they would grin with reflected light every night until Halloween. The town *became* Halloween.

In Rainer Park, the tents for the week-long festival were poled into place, aired out, made ready. In the huge exhibition tent, tables were lined into aisles, and were filled with everything pumpkin related imaginable: foods of all kinds, pumpkin goods (pumpkin colored slippers for Dad, pumpkin colored terry robes for Mom) and pumpkin services (THE BEST ROTOTILLER IN THE WORLD! one booth, perhaps fibbing, proclaimed). Bunting was orange and black, crepe paper everywhere, orange mostly, big fat pumpkin lamps overhead smiling down on the expected crowd, making the tent (orange and white striped itself) glow like the inside of a huge pumpkin.

The other huge tent, offering a week's worth of music entertainment, also orange and white striped, went up nearby: one night of bluegrass, one of soft rock, one hard rock, one rap, one country, one classical, and one (heaven forbid) talent night, anything goes.

There would be pumpkin rolling races, pumpkin carving contests, a pumpkin catapult shootout (Mr. Clark's high school physics class inevitably took that prize), the pumpkin weigh-in, the beauty pageant which would crown Ms. Pumpkin Days, a pumpkin pie eating contest (which, one rueful year, had turned into a pumpkin pie throwing contest—again thanks to Mr. Clark's physics class), pumpkin cook-offs, recipe swaps, a prize for The Most Unusual Use of a Pumpkin (shoes, the previous year), a hundred other celebrations public and private (sometimes too private: there was, for instance, the year when Deputy Sheriff Charlie Fredericks discovered one of the Lund boys deep in the recesses of Rainer Park doing something with the carved eye hole of a pumpkin—but never mind) of Orangefield's most illustrious and profitable product. The Mayor would speak; a congressman would speak; there was, every year, the perpetual rumor, which proved to be just that, that a former president would speak.

The culmination of a year's worth of work and commerce, the Pumpkin Days Festival would, for an entire week, turn Orangefield orange. It would, as always, prove to the world that Orangefield was, indeed, the world capital for pumpkins, that it was a very special place with a very special history.

For one week, Orangefield was the most wonderful place in the world.

And, during that week, something stirred.

Something stirred . . .

Chapter Seventeen

The black cape was back.

There was a man in it, Marvin Soames was pretty sure—but that fella sure as hell didn't want to be seen. The cape kept swirling back and forth, and the man's face, if it was a face, was pasty white and hardly there. The body was worse—a wisp of something inside the cape that looked as if it would break apart if you breathed on it.

Which was not something Marvin wanted to get close enough to do.

You awake, Marvin?

The voice, as always, was inside Marvin's head, though it sounded as though it came from the face in the cape.

Marvin grunted a noncommittal sound.

You with me? Get up, Marvin.

Marvin grunted again, but rolled off his side onto his back and pulled himself into a sullen sitting position. Not wise to ignore The Voice. He'd done it once, and paid for it: the runs for three days, and a belly that felt like it was on fire. If he played ball, on the other hand, there was often something . . .

"Bring anything for your ol' pal?" Marvin said, cocking one eye at the cape, which swirled closer to him. A smell there: empty and cold, like going into a dirt cellar in the heat of summer.

You'll find it where you always do, Marvin. I do take care of you, don't I?

Marvin snuffled. " 'Cept for that time you burned my belly up—"

The Voice laughed. *Nobody made you drink it, Marvin. And you do have a long memory.*

"Goddam rotgut wood alcohol. I never forget nothin' that's been done to me."

That's good. Because I have a job for you, and I want you to remember just such a thing.

Ignoring the cape, Marvin got up and shuffled to the tree behind The Voice. Sure enough, there was a bottle in a bag. He pulled it out—a pretty decent bottle of white wine.

"Need a corkscrew for this one," he said sullenly, trying to hide his pleasure. If there was a job to do he might be able to get another bottle out of it.

In his hands there was a tug on the bottle; as he watched, the foil peeled away from the top and the cork slid up and, with a pop, was pulled free.

He looked at the cape, which had nearly fallen

to the ground—a wisp of something left his side and then the cape was swirling and flapping again.

And another if you do what I ask.

"I'll think about it," he answered, already calculating that perhaps *two* more bottles could be negotiated.

Don't get greedy, Marvin.

The bottle in his hands, just as he was bringing it to his mouth, turned boiling hot and he dropped it with a shout. The palms of his hands showed angry red welts.

"I—"

Here's what I want you to do, Marvin. Now . . .

Riley Gates had discovered long ago that people were slobs. Even in a pick-your-own-pumpkin patch they managed to leave all kinds of trash—tissues and soda cans, even used baby diapers. Once Riley had found the leavings of a complete chicken dinner for four. And he'd also found that if he didn't keep the place clean, the same slobs wouldn't come back the next year.

His back ached from all the bending over, and his feet hurt, but after stowing the trash in the can he kept at the edge of the field he was able to sit in the lawn chair he had there next to his weighing station and cash box and relax. It was late in the day, almost time to close up, but there were still a few customers about—a family with five kids marching toward him now—each kid had a pumpkin relative to his size in reverse order. The biggest kid, who Riley estimated to be twelve—she had that bored, what am I doing here look on her face that would only get worse—held the smallest and the littlest kid, in the neighborhood of three, had both arms around a monster that he could hardly see over.

"Well, now, sure you can handle that, podna?" Riley laughed, trying to help the child with his burden. But he wouldn't let go.

"Give it to me! Give it to me!" he shouted, when Riley tried to lift the pumpkin out of his hands.

"Gotta weigh it, podna, to see how much it costs!"

He gripped it tighter, his face screwing up in effort.

The boy's father said, "Sorry. We've been trying to get him to let go of it for ten minutes, but he says it's the perfect pumpkin and nobody else is going to get it." He nodded his head wearily at his other kids.

"Well, now," Riley said, rubbing his chin. "How much does he weigh?"

Without hesitation, the boy's haggard mother said, "Forty-two pounds."

Riley nodded. "Fair enough." With a grunt, he bent down, instantly regretting it, and lifted both boy and pumpkin up onto the scale.

"Weighs just a shade over fifty, now. We'll call it eight pounds even."

To his relief he watched the boy's father help his son down.

Riley spent the next five minutes weighing the other pumpkins, including the one carried by the twelve-year-old girl who said, to no one in particular, "Can we *go* now?"

Riley waved them off, closing his cash box, and entertained a few secret thoughts about big families and parental discipline. He shook his head and sat back down in his chair with a grunt.

There was only one customer left in the field, and he seemed to be spending a long time rooted to a single spot. Riley watched him for a while, then lost interest and picked up the paperback mystery he was reading.

In five minutes, when he looked up, the man was still bent over the same spot.

Riley tried to go back to the mystery novel, but finally gave up, concentrating on the customer. If he didn't move soon . . .

The man finally straightened, then bent down again, as if examining the ground.

Riley hauled himself out of his chair and sauntered over, favoring his aching feet.

"Havin' trouble deciding?" he said amiably.

The man stood up, but kept his back to Riley.

Gates drew up close to him. "I said, podna—"

The man turned around, and Riley saw something flash in the late day sun—the long edge of a blade that punched into his middle. For a few seconds there was no sensation, and then a burning began, which went up his spine—

"Marvin Soames—" Riley gasped, and the other man stepped forward, driving the blade deeper.

"Sure as hell is, Detective Gates," Soames said into Riley's face as he pushed the knife in to the hilt. His breath smelled like alcohol. He followed Riley over and back as the big man collapsed to the ground, and straddled his middle, still driving and moving the knife. "Sure as hell is. I don't forget nothin', and I don't forget what you did to me."

Riley was fighting for breath, and the heat was driving up into his head. "You . . ." he gasped. "You . . ."

"Let me say it for you, fat man," Marvin hissed. "You arrested me for vagrancy, and you arrested me for public nuisance. I did ten days for each. I never forgot."

"But . . . this . . ." Riley said.

"I got a friend asked a favor," Soames said. He edged the blade up, keeping pressure on it.

Behind Marvin Soames, something cut off the lowering sun. It was black, and moved more than the breeze should cause it to—a cape, hanging in mid air, with something barely seen filling it . . .

"Sam . . . Samhain . . ." Riley gasped.

That's right, Mr. Gates. That file of yours was a big one. I thought we should meet.

"But . . ."

Riley screamed as Marvin Soames yanked the blade up through his middle another inch.

When the fire cleared from Gates's eyes, he saw the pale, ashy outline of a face with no eyes just in front of him. The mouth was empty blackness.

"Wh . . ." Riley tried to get out.

You've become a bother, Mr. Gates. You could get in the way of certain plans. If you were to ask me why, that's what I would answer . . .

Riley fought for breath, felt a copper taste in his mouth, could no longer see.

But actually, Samhain said, *if you were to ask me why, I would answer: "Why not?"*

Chapter Eighteen

For the hundredth time in the last few days, Corrie checked the telephoto lens set up in the guest room trained on the cornfield. But the scarecrow was not there. The light of a waxing moon showed an empty pole where the pumpkin-headed man had been. Corrie kept expecting John to show up—to feel the sudden crackly, feathery weight of his arm thrown around his shoulder, or to turn around and have the grinning pumpkin mouth there. But there had been no further visits. In a bizarre way Corrie was disappointed, as if an old acquaintance had suddenly vanished without leaving a forwarding address.

And John had said things would get much worse . . .

So far, nothing had happened that Corrie hadn't experienced in the past. Growing up, he had become almost accustomed to the occasional odd noise, the shifting geometries in walls and ceilings, the sudden plasticity of a piece of furniture or the floor beneath his feet. The fact that others, including his mother, could at most hear a particularly loud noise but could see none of the things he saw had become normal to him.

This was his world, and welcome to it.

He swiveled the telephoto lens away from the cornfield, toward Orangefield. The town was lit up like a lantern. The beginning of Pumpkin Days, and they could keep all of it. He had gone out that afternoon for some groceries, and couldn't find a parking spot. Finally he had parked in front of a fire hydrant, and gotten a ticket for his trouble.

He would stay away from town for the next week . . .

Through the lens he could see some of the decorated light poles, the flash of a strobe set up outside Rainer park, which threw a light deep into the sky, illuminating the scant clouds like a horizontal movie screen with the grinning happy face of a pumpkin . . .

There, on the ground next to the strobe, was a figure who resembled John . . .

It was gone the next moment, lost in the milling crowds.

There was a noise behind Corrie, and he turned, half expecting the Pumpkin man to be there—

"John?"

GET UP TO
4 FREE BOOKS!

You can have the best fiction delivered to your door for less
than what you'd pay in a bookstore or online—only $4.25 a book!
Sign up for our book clubs today, and we'll send you **FREE* BOOKS**
just for trying it out...with **no obligation to buy, ever!**

LEISURE HORROR BOOK CLUB

With more award-winning horror authors than any other publisher, it's
easy to see why CNN.com says "Leisure Books has been leading the way
in paperback horror novels." Your shipments will include authors such as
RICHARD LAYMON, DOUGLAS CLEGG, JACK KETCHUM, MARY ANN MITCHELL,
and many more.

LEISURE THRILLER BOOK CLUB

If you love fast-paced page-turners, you won't want to miss any of the books
in Leisure's thriller line. Filled with gripping tension and edge-of-your-seat
excitement, these titles feature everything from psychological suspense to
legal thrillers to police procedurals and more!

As a book club member you also receive the following special benefits:
30% OFF all orders through our website & telecenter!
Exclusive access to special discounts!
**Convenient home delivery and 10 days to return any
books you don't want to keep.**

There is no **minimum number of books to buy**, and you may cancel
membership at any time. See back to sign up!

*Please include $2.00 for shipping and handling.

YES! ☐

Sign me up for the Leisure Horror Book Club and send my TWO FREE BOOKS! If I choose to stay in the club, I will pay only $8.50* each month, a savings of $5.48!

YES! ☐

Sign me up for the Leisure Thriller Book Club and send my TWO FREE BOOKS! If I choose to stay in the club, I will pay only $8.50* each month, a savings of $5.48!

NAME: _____

ADDRESS: _____

_____

TELEPHONE: _____

E-MAIL: _____

☐ **I WANT TO PAY BY CREDIT CARD.**

☐   ☐ MasterCard ☐ DISCOVER

ACCOUNT #: _____

EXPIRATION DATE: _____

SIGNATURE: _____

Send this card along with $2.00 shipping & handling for each club you wish to join, to:

Horror/Thriller Book Clubs
1 Mechanic Street
Norwalk, CT 06850-3431

Or fax (must include credit card information!) to: 610.995.9274. You can also sign up online at www.dorchesterpub.com.

*Plus $2.00 for shipping. Offer open to residents of the U.S. and Canada only. Canadian residents please call 1.800.481.9191 for pricing information.

If under 18, a parent or guardian must sign. Terms, prices and conditions subject to change. Subscription subject to acceptance. Dorchester Publishing reserves the right to reject any order or cancel any subscription.

There was nothing—empty hallway illuminated by a nightlight.

Another sound—from down below, on the first floor.

Corrie left the telephoto lens, walked out into the hallway, stood at the top of the stairs.

"Hello?" he said.

Silence—then that sound again: something straining, like two nailed pieces of wood being pried apart—

"Who's down there?"

He expected John's voice—but there was only dead silence followed by that peculiar creaking sound.

He quickly dismounted the stairs, checked the front door (closed and locked) and went into the kitchen (nothing), the dining room (nothing), the living room—

The sound came again, startlingly loud, in the direction of the sofa against the wall.

As he touched the couch, the sound came again from behind it.

Corrie switched on the table lamp next to the sofa, and inched it away from the wall.

He saw nothing. Then the creaking sound came again and his eyes instantly focused on the baseboard molding. Where two pieces met, one of them was straining away from the wall. Something like a black hairy finger was poking out from behind the wall.

The straining sound again—and now the finger thrust out farther into the room, becoming thicker, matted with long, midnight-black strands of hair.

A mighty heave, and part of the sheet rock at the base of the wall cracked outward. The finger jutted farther, becoming thicker and thicker, forcing the sofa farther away from the wall.

A second finger appeared beside the first, extending—

The hole widened. Another finger, and yet another appeared, prying the sheet rock aside as the first black fingers, now three feet long, jointed with slick black knuckles, resolved into jointed legs—

There was a horrid sucking sound and more legs, followed by a huge bulbous body, popped out of the hole in the wall. Now a creature resembling a spider, nearly five feet wide, stood panting behind the couch. Two ruby eyes regarded Corrie maliciously. Already it was nudging the sofa aside, advancing on him.

Corrie stumbled backwards and reached for the table lamp. As its cord was pulled from the wall the room went darker, the red eyes of the spider thing like tight stoked coals, its mouth rasping like a bellows as it crawled forward toward him.

Corrie gasped and took a swing as the spider lurched at him, feinted one way then crouched and lunged outward, low and left. Corrie, still backing away, hit the entryway to the living room and stumbled back into the hall. The spider followed, balancing on all legs save two, which it thrust out in front of it, trying to gouge at him first low, then high. Corrie fended off the attacks, but now found himself on the stairs leading to the upper rooms.

He threw the lamp, turned, ran up the stairs, stumbled and fell halfway, felt the thick hairy appendages of the spider on his feet, moving up his legs.

He turned on the stairs and kicked outward. The spider hissed, backed away, then lunged; Corrie kicked with both feet, driving it aside and, as it screeched and fell back, he crawled to his feet and ran up the stairs and into the guest room.

The walls were gone, the doorknob disappearing in his hand. He was on a flat dark plain, endless in all directions, a single brightness at one horizon which looked like the rising sun but, as it brightened, became the spider in negative image, shining gray-white, even more horrid, one eye, now green, glowing balefully as it scuttled at him across the plain. The other eye pulsed palely as it hung like a broken egg yolk from the thing's face.

Corrie turned and ran—

—and hit a wall, as the guest room returned. He fell, stunned, to the ground, listening for the monster.

There was silence again in the house.

After a time, arming himself with a curtain rod, he cautiously opened the door and looked out.

The hallway was empty, the stairway empty.

Tensed to run or fight, he slowly descended the stairs and looked into the living room.

The sofa was back in position, the lamp on its table.

He inched his way in, pulled the sofa away from the wall.

The wall was undamaged, the clamshell molding in place.

Corrie's breathing slowly returned to normal.

He pushed the sofa back into place.

And noticed the long scratches down his arms—one of them a deep gouge filled with blood.

One leg of his pants was shredded, another gouge in his leg, deeper than the other.

They had not gone away.

The wounds were real.

He felt real pain, not illusion.

Things will only get worse, John had said.

Now, dreams and reality were melding.

Chapter Nineteen

Grant was going to say, "I want to know all about weird shit," but when the door opened—and it was an extremely strange door, dark orange, with a stained glass pumpkin set into the half circle that topped it; the house itself dark and gloomy, surrounded by dead, fallen trees and live ones in dire need of trimming—and he was faced with an attractive young woman, dark hair, doe eyes, who looked as frightened as anyone he'd ever seen, he kept his mouth shut.

"May I help you?" she asked, in a faint voice tinged with a heavy accent.

Grant took his cigarette from his mouth, showed his badge, said, "I was hoping to speak to someone about Thomas Reynolds's work."

"He was my husband. He's dead."

"I know," Grant said. "I thought perhaps someone else in the household . . ."

"You would want my son," she said, and opened the door to let him in.

Grant threw down his cigarette and toed it out on the front step.

The inside of the house was even gloomier than the outside. It was much too dark, for one thing. The entry led into a hallway lit only by a pumpkin-shaped sconce; there was a piece of furniture in the hall that looked like a carved wooden skull with a hinged open cranium; it was lined with felt and empty. The pictures on the walls were dark, tossed-sea images and small houses surrounded by hills under threatening skies, and the living room she led him into looked like a funeral parlor from a horror film. The sofa was upholstered in black or dark blue fabric, flanked by two red damask chairs and fronted by an ebony coffee table. The fireplace, filled with ashes, looked like it hadn't been used in some time. Above it were three stuffed animals: a field mouse, chipmunk, and, best of all, a squirrel, which had been mounted on its hind legs in an attack pose, complete with open mouth and wild eyes.

Grant almost said, "I don't believe this," but, again, kept his mouth shut.

"Is there anything in particular you wanted to know about my husband?" his hostess asked; she hadn't offered her name or her hand or her hospitality. She stood in the entry to the living room, hugging herself as if she were cold.

"And your name is . . . ?" Grant asked, deciding that acting official was the best course of action.

She hesitated a moment. "Anja." She spelled it for him. "Anja Reynolds."

Grant thought he had her accent pegged. "You're Russian?"

Again a hesitation, and Grant suddenly had her figured out.

"I'm not from the INS," he said. "I'm just a local cop, trying to get some information."

Instantly, she warmed a bit, though she still wouldn't come into the room and continued to hug herself. "You are like that other man who was here earlier this year, Mr. Gates?"

"I'm a friend of his."

She nodded. "As I told Mr. Gates, my husband and I were married in London, and there was some question about my status here, even though my son was born in America. I'm afraid—"

"Not from me," Grant said. He smiled, and took out a cigarette, only to put it back in the pack when she frowned. "Can I talk to your son?"

"Certainly. Please." She motioned that he should sit, but instead of coming into the room herself she disappeared into the recesses of the house. Grant heard the distant deep *tick tick* of what he guessed to be a grandfather clock. A heavy door was opened with a creak. He heard muffled conversation. Then the door was closed again.

Grant sat on one of the damask chairs, which

proved to be so uncomfortable that he moved to the couch, which was even worse. He had never liked Sheridan sofas—one had a tendency to slide off them.

He was about to go back to the damask chair when a boy of about thirteen strode into the room. He looked like a miniature man. He was dressed in a white shirt and tie, dark slacks, cordovan loafers. He wore spectacles—Grant couldn't call them eyeglasses they were so round and old-fashioned looking—and his hair was slicked back with what proved to be Vaseline when Grant later got a whiff of it. Behind the spectacles he had guppy eyes, large and goggling. He didn't smile. Under one arm he carried a large portfolio, which he placed gently on the ebony coffee table.

Then he stepped back, and bowed!

Grant didn't know what to say. He took out his notebook and flipped it open.

"Alright if I write some of this down?" he said, in a neutral voice—he didn't know whether to treat this creature like a boy, a man, or a headwaiter.

"That would be fine," the boy said, in clipped, accented English. His diction was too perfect.

"Would you sit down and help me?" Grant offered.

The boy bowed again and sat stiffly in the damask chair Grant had abandoned.

Grant became aware of another presence, and turned slightly to see the boy's mother, just outside the room, standing in the gloom of the hallway with her arms folded, watching them.

"Doesn't your mother like this room?" Grant asked, loud enough for her to hear.

The boy blinked. "No. She's afraid. It was there"—he pointed to an ornate table on the far side of the room, which held an old fashioned rotary telephone—"that my father died. All that was found was a pile of bones."

Grant was startled to see a flare of excitement in the boy's face.

"Aren't *you* afraid to come in here?" Grant probed.

"I find it fascinating." His voice was so perfect it sounded robotic. "I find everything to do with this house, this town, fascinating. She"—he raised his voice at the word and looked quickly toward his mother and then back at Grant—"does not."

"I see." Grant indicated the portfolio. "And what's that?"

"The answer to all your questions, I imagine. It is the second volume of my father's occult history of Orangefield. I trust you've read the first volume, *Occult Practices in Orangefield and Chicawa County, New York, 1668–1940?*"

"Actually, no."

"You should start there." He abruptly rose, and retrieved the portfolio from the table, placing it firmly under his arm. "This will do you no good until you've read volume one. Volume two is unpublished." He stood as stiff and proud as a toy soldier. "Someday *I* will write volume three."

He marched to the hallway; Grant was interested to see that his mother had disappeared. The boy stopped and turned around.

"I must tell you, Detective Grant, that you will examine this volume at your own risk." He held it out, and at the same time lowered his voice. "Samhain himself told my father not to publish it, though it was ready for the printer. My father followed his instructions, but then betrayed Samhain at the last minute. Hence . . ."

He looked toward the ornate telephone table again.

At the mention of Samhain, Grant thought of Riley Gates. "So you believe Samhain is real?"

Again that flush of excitement on the boy's pale face. He nearly ran back to the coffee table, placed the portfolio carefully back down and sat back down in the damask chair.

He leaned forward, his eyes nearly popping through their spectacle lenses. "Mr. Grant, you must understand that the history of Orangefield, for the most part, *is* the history of Samhain. He's been here at least since the early 1940s, and possibly earlier. My own theory is that he was here long before that, but not very active. Much of volume three will concern this prequel era, as well as more recent manifestations."

"When I was a kid there were so-called Sammy sightings, but we never took it very seriously—"

"You should have! He's been very crafty, and very selective. If he hasn't come much to the attention of the police in all these years, think of how sly he is."

The boy looked pretty sly himself, entertaining himself, Grant thought, with private ghoulish fantasies.

The boy looked at him boldly, and leaned even closer.

"You do know who Samhain is, don't you?"

"The Lord of the Dead? By the way, what do you like to be called: Tom? Thomas?"

"Thomas, Jr., would be fine."

"We'll keep it at Thomas, if it's all right with you."

The boy nodded. "And Samhain is not merely 'The Lord of the Dead.' He was, first and foremost, a Celtic figure. The common conception was that, on All Hallows Eve, he had the power to bring the dead back to life for that one evening. But this is a gross simplification. The word Samhain was originally dedicated to a festival, not to a god. To the Celts, the festival of Samhain celebrated the end of one year and the beginning of the next—in essence, the death of one cycle and, hopefully, the beginning of a new one. For that one evening, October thirty-first, the spirits of all those who died the previous year would roam the earth. The Celts sought to ward them off with offerings of food and drink. They also maintained hilltop sacrificial sites, where animals and humans would be burned alive. This was all in hopes that the ground would renew after the winter and guarantee good crops in the new year."

The boy's eyes were nearly on fire with excitement. Grant realized that he hadn't taken any notes; he badly wanted a cigarette. Out of the corner of his eye he could see the boy's mother once again stationed in the entryway to the room, hugging herself.

"The Romans adopted many of the Samhain festivities, incorporating them into one of their own holidays; later in the ninth century Pope Gregory IV tried to replace it altogether with All Saints Day. But before All Saints Day came All Souls Day, so the idea of the Day of Death remained. And eventually the ritual Samhain became the figure Samhain, the Lord of the Dead who ruled over what eventually evolved into Halloween. There were some French influences, too . . ." The boy waved his hand in dismissal.

"And Samhain ended up in Orangefield?" Grant said.

The boy jumped up, startling both Grant and his mother in the entryway, who flinched. "Yes! But we don't know how, or why. Not yet, anyway. I intend to find out. But that isn't the greatest mystery, or danger, with Samhain . . ."

Grant waited, but the boy merely sat down, drawing the portfolio off the coffee table and holding it on his lap with his hands folded on top of it.

"That would be . . . ?" Grant said, after a few moments of silence.

The mother had moved off; Grant could hear her steps receding quickly down the hallway into the back of the house; there came a muffled slam of a door.

The boy shook his head. Grant noticed that his hands were trembling.

The boy was staring at Grant intently. The detective had seen it before, in suspects: the need to talk battling mightily with the fear of doing so.

"Are you afraid?" Grant asked.

The boy made no movement, then nodded curtly.

Grant got up, stiffly, making a noise. "Then maybe I should be going. Thanks for your time—"

The boy was at his elbow instantly. "Please stay," he said in a fierce whisper.

Grant settled back down onto the uncomfortable sofa, pushing himself back over the slippery cushions.

"There's another one," the boy said, barely loud enough to whisper.

"Another what?" Grant offered.

"Samhain, for all his power over the dead, is only a servant. He only does what he's told to do . . ."

Grant waited. The boy's mother was back; Grant heard her crying out in the hallway. Then her voice, muffled, frightened, called the boy's name: "Thomas, Jr." She pronounced it "Toe-mass," and there was pleading in it.

"That's all I can tell you, detective." The boy got up, the portfolio once more in place under his arm.

Grant rose, too. "If I come back after reading your father's book, will you show me the second volume? We'll talk some more?"

The boy turned at the entryway. "Come back then," he said. And bowed and turned away.

His steps echoed down the hallway.

Grant was prepared to let himself out, but the boy's mother was there when he left the living room. She grabbed his arm.

"Detective—"

Grant's cell phone went off, and he reached into his jacket pocket for it, rooting past his cigarette pack and other detritus. He drew it out and turned it on.

"Excuse me," he said to Mrs. Reynolds.

"Grant here," he said into the phone, and listened. He kept listening, as he went numb.

"*My God*," he said.

Chapter Twenty

It was time for a monkey conference.

The concept was simple and elegant. And it worked. It had worked for Marcia Bright's family when she was growing up, and she had adopted it for her own husband and daughter, with similar results.

This was how it worked: everyone in the family was given a stuffed animal, a monkey of their own choosing, and whenever something needed to be discussed as a family, a monkey conference was called. Everyone arrived at the kitchen table with their monkey (which made it official) and the conference began.

This time, there were only two participants at the monkey conference. Gina had been put to bed, and Marcia herself, for the first time, forgot to bring her stuffed monkey—the same sock creature she had used as a child—to the table.

"Marcia, there's nothing wrong with her," Ted began. His own stuffed animal sat on the floor next to his chair.

"The doctor gave her a thorough check-up," Marcia agreed.

"Maybe you—"

"There's nothing wrong with *me*, Ted! Just because you sleep like a rock, and haven't heard any of these noises at night, or during the daytime because you're at work."

"Nothing happened last weekend while I was home—though, if you remember, you had me up all night listening."

She said nothing.

He tried to remain reasonable. "Do you really think our house is suddenly . . . *haunted*? And that these . . . playmates of hers are real?"

She glared at him. "Don't patronize me."

He threw up his hands. "We've lived here seven years, and now the house is *possessed*?"

"It's not the house—it's Gina. And it's Corrie Phaeder's fault."

There came a faint sound from above, and they paused; Ted followed his wife's eyes to the ceiling while they both listened: a creak.

"House settling for the night," Ted offered.

"Maybe," Marcia answered.

"Look," Ted said, continuing their conversation, "what exactly is it you want me to do? Hire an exorcist?"

"I want you to talk to the police, and make them

do something about our neighbor." There was steel in her voice.

Ted threw up his hands in exasperation. "Do *what?* Put a stake through his heart? Shoot him with a silver bullet? Drive him out of town with torches? How 'bout if I talk to this weirdo, man to man—"

Something about the way his wife was looking at him, some seriousness of purpose he had never seen before, made him stop. When he spoke again his voice was filled with concern. "Marsh, are you okay?"

His wife whispered hoarsely, "Don't you hear it?"

There *was* a sound, which had been building in the back of Ted's hearing, and now rose to the forefront—a sound like a dripping of water from a great height—there was a *drip drip* followed by two deep splashing sounds, which was getting louder and louder—

"What in blazes—"

Ted rose from the kitchen table, kicking his stuffed monkey, a large brown one, aside and walking to the stairs.

"Do you think the faucet upstairs, the shower—?"

The sound was growing and growing, way beyond what a plumbing problem would cause.

He moved up the stairs, two at a time, Marcia close behind him.

"What the—"

A bright light, like a strobe was flashing out from beneath their daughter's bedroom door. As

Ted reached for the knob the door flew open, blinding him.

"Gina!" he called.

There was no sound, and he thrust his way into the room.

The light was instantly extinguished, and now he heard his daughter calling for him and Marcia.

"Mommy! Daddy!"

She was wide awake, in the middle of the rug on the floor, flopping as if riding an invisible horse. She looked in their direction but Ted could tell she couldn't see them.

"Mommy, make the ocean go away!"

They heard a huge creak, like a huge wooden ship being tossed by waves; the sound of a monstrous storm, lightning and thunder and the crash of water, filled the room.

"Mommmmmeeeee!"

Their daughter was thrown into the air, then stopped suspended about two feet above the floor; she floundered, flailing her arms and crying.

"Mommeee! I can't swim!"

She began to sink toward the floor, gasping for breath as if her mouth were filling with water.

Marcia jumped forward and grabbed her.

"Ted!"

He knelt beside his daughter as she was lowered to the floor, fighting for breath.

"Ted, do something!"

Not knowing what else to do, he put his mouth

154

over his daughter's and tried to push air into her lungs—to his horror her mouth felt as if it was filled with water.

"*My God, my God—*"

Gina was turning blue, convulsing, trying to fight her way to an invisible surface.

Marcia lifted her daughter up, raising her more than two feet off the ground.

Gina suddenly heaved like a fish and began to gulp air.

Ted took her from his wife and held her higher.

Something blinked in the room, shifted like a lens shutter being snapped—and suddenly everything was back to normal.

The noises disappeared like a tone-arm being pulled from a phonograph record.

Gina gave a huge, trembling sigh, and was instantly asleep.

Ted stood in shocked silence, holding his daughter aloft as if she were a trophy, while his wife, breathing heavily, stared at him.

He slowly lowered Gina into his wife's arms.

There was a moment of silence.

"I'll talk to Phaeder," he said.

From somewhere far away, Corrie heard banging. He thought it was part of his dream. But there had been no sound like that the day he met Kathy Marks. It had been raining, in summer, and the clouds had just parted and everything was wet and the sky turned deep blue almost in a heartbeat. The air smelled like after-rain, fresh and dry-wet, like a curtain pulled aside from storm to calm. There was the sound of dripping water from the tree leaves.

"You come here a lot?" he said, startling her. She was standing at the edge of the picnic area, staring at a tree, and he thought she was watching the water drip from the green leaves.

"I don't like Rainer Park," she answered, after looking at him, perhaps judging him in that instant and then dismissing him.

"I know I'm younger than you are, but—"

"Wanted to see the freak?" she said, not turning around. He had never heard anyone speak so bitterly.

"No. I—"

She pointed. "That's the tree. You can still see the mark on the branch the rope made, if you get up close."

He stood squinting where she indicated.

"Do you look at it a lot?"

She said nothing, and he turned around to go, thinking it a lost cause, until she suddenly said, her voice dropping a tone: "All the time."

She turned around to study him more closely. "You're Corrie Something, right?"

"Phaeder."

She nodded slowly, her eyes still on him. "Big house on Sagett River. Your father took off when you were little."

He didn't know what else to say, so he shrugged and said, "That's me."

"Why did you follow me here?"

"*I didn't—*"

"*Don't give me that—I saw you following me today, and yesterday, and Thursday last week.*"

"*It was Friday.*"

"*It was Thursday. Think about it.*" She was still frowning, her eyes looking him over like a caught bug.

He concentrated. "*You're right, it was Thursday.*"

"*No it wasn't. It was actually Friday. I wanted to see if you would lie so I wouldn't send you away.*"

"*I—*" he had no idea what to say or do.

"*I take it you're not a big hit with the girls,*" she said, and for the first time he sensed her melt a bit. The frown was gone, leaving her features smooth but blank. He wondered how pretty she would look when she smiled. She had all the right features for prettiness, but there was nothing to light them up.

He wanted to light them up, but had no idea how to do that.

"*I like you,*" he finally blurted out.

The frown was back, in spades. "*You're three years younger than me,*" she said, and turned to consider the oak tree again. The freshened air was turning summer warm again, the cool wet misting back to humidity. Dappled sunlight made leaf shadows race in tight circles on the ground.

"*I—strange things happen to me,*" he said. "*I see things, and hear things in my head.*"

She turned sharply, and now he felt as if he was being dissected. "*Then you're nuts. Or lying.*"

And then he began to cry.

157

When the tears stopped, she was standing near him, staring at him in amazement. He sniffled and cleared his eyes. She held a crumpled tissue out to him.

"Use this," she ordered.

He finished the job, and handed the tissue back to her. He felt as if he should leave, run away, but he was rooted to the spot by the possibility of what she would say next.

"I never saw a fifteen-year-old boy cry before," she said.

"Sorry."

"It's all right. It proves you're not completely full of it."

Abruptly she turned away from him, and away from the tree, and began to walk to one of the picnic tables at the far end of the clearing.

"Sit down. Let's talk," she said.

Two hours later, they were friends.

He told her everything, and she told him everything, even if most of it was known. When they had exhausted their obvious troubles, they talked about school, which would start again in three weeks—Kathy would be a senior, and Corrie a freshman.

"I suggest you don't try that crying act when you're a frosh," she counseled. "They'll pound you senseless."

"I don't plan on it." He was still waiting for her first smile, though she had come close.

"I suppose you let everything out because it was the first time you could. Like it was all bottled up, the cork waiting to pop."

"Something like that."

She looked at him closely. "I think you'll be all right. You can always come to me if you need help. Not that I'm popular at all—they call me Bookworm. But that's okay, because I want to be a librarian after I get out of school. I've started looking at colleges that teach library science."

The prospect of losing this friend he had just made cast Corrie into gloom.

"Hey, it's all right! It's a long way away. And what about you? What do you want to do?"

"I like photography."

She nodded approval. "That might get you out of this town, which is what you need to do. Me too. Who knows, maybe we'll leave together."

"Fine with me."

Then she smiled, which made her face flush like an angel.

And he fell in love with her.

Eventually, she fell in love with him. It was almost a year later, in the summer week before she was to leave for college, that they both admitted it.

The afternoon started out with a picnic lunch, away from the picnic tables, which were being used by a bratty group of five-year-olds and their parents for a birthday party. They went deeper into the back part of Rainer Park, behind the picnic area, where the ground was covered in pine needles and the trees were a forest of old Christmas against the autumn sky. They found a soft spot in a small clearing and laid out their blanket and then ate chicken and cold potato salad and drank iced-tea in near silence.

Something was strange. Corrie knew it. It had been building for weeks, and it had something to do with Kathy leaving. But it was more than that. When she looked at him something was different about her eyes. It was as if they had become deeper pools, pulling him in after them.

He was afraid to touch her.

"I'll be home in October, for Columbus Day weekend,"
she said. "Already got a bus ticket." They were the first
words she had said in a while, and they sounded hollow.

He nodded.

"Someone told me to get bus tickets way in advance,
'cause the seats sell out fast, especially around holidays.
I'll probably get my Thanksgiving ticket first week I'm
up there."

Corrie wiped his hands, put the remains of his last
chicken leg into the empty bucket.

She turned those deep pools of eyes on him.

"I want you to be here when I come back."

"I will be."

She leaned over, pushing the bucket aside, and kissed
him. "I want you to be here."

And then it was like an electric switch had been
thrown. They moved the remains of the food off the
blanket, and straightened it somewhat, and then they
were out of their clothes and fumbling with each other
and then, suddenly, they got it right. It was over almost
before it began. But later Corrie remembered that the
sun through the trees didn't look the same afterwards,
the light was different, the feel of the ground under-
neath him different, the sounds of the distant birthday

*party filtering through from the picnic grounds differ-
ent. The day even smelled different, autumn-cool and at
the same time sun-warm.*

*He lay back with his hands behind his head and
stared at the gently swaying branches of the trees; a leaf
from a nearby oak broke away from its branch, dying,
vivid red, and slowly pirouetted down at him.*

*Kathy's face loomed over him, blocking out the trees,
the sky—*

"Now you own me," she said. "And I own you."

*He opened his mouth to say something, but covered it
with a sound as if something was stuck in his throat and
said nothing.*

*Later, when he was alone, he thought about what she
had said and it frightened and thrilled him at the same
time.*

*Kathy did not last the semester at school, and when she
came home something had changed. Not with her—she
was the same as when she had left, as ardent in her need
for him. Something had changed in Corrie, and she
knew it immediately.*

*He did not come to see her. When she called him re-
peatedly, getting no answer, she finally went to his
house. She knew he was there, could feel his presence behind the door, the shaded windows. She heard noises,
deep rumblings and stirrings and other sounds of his
captivity. Angered, she found a rock near the front walk
and threw it at his window, missing but hitting the
shutter with a* clack.

He came to the door then, opened it and came out.

He looked very tired and disheveled. He would not look at her.

"It's been very bad, in the house."

"Where's your mother?"

"At work."

"I thought we made a pact that we would help each other."

He nodded, looked at the ground, said nothing.

"Corrie, the deal was that we help each other."

"I'm sorry I haven't been there for you—"

"I'm talking about you, Corrie. You need help."

"I'm coping," he said.

She was filled with anger. "You're not! When was the last time you slept?"

A wry smile flitted across his face. "A while ago. When I sleep I dream as if I'm awake. When I'm awake . . ." He shrugged, turning to look back into the house."

"Corrie, let me help you."

"I'll manage—"

He took a step back into the house, and she reached out and held his arm. He looked down at her hand as if he had never seen it before.

"I have to go back in—"

"Let me go with you."

He focused on her. "That wouldn't be wise. It doesn't want you to. It told me to make you go away."

"It can't stop me—"

She took a firm step forward, but now Corrie's hands were on her, holding her back.

"Go away, Kathy."

She resisted, trying to step into the house.

Suddenly he slapped her, and a series of rattles and a thumping boom sounded inside.

Startled, Kathy put her hand to her cheek where he had hit her.

"I'm . . . sorry . . ." he said, moving past her into the house. He closed the door and she heard the click of the lock and then the slide of a bolt.

She stood staring at the door, and her hand fell to her side.

"But I need you!" she shouted once, at the mute door.

She went to school nearby, earning her library science degree. Corrie was now a senior. They saw each occasionally, always at her instigation, and there were more awkward silences, no intimate moments.

"I love you," she told him one night that summer, af-ter a nearly silent dinner. They sat in her car in front of his house.

The silence in the car was a live thing.

"I don't know what to say to you," he said, finally. Then he added: "Yes, I do. We made a deal always to be honest. I think you fell in love with me to take the place of that voice in your head that made you try to kill your-self. You want me to take the place of that voice and tell you what to do. I can't do that, Kathy."

"That's not true."

"I think it is. I think that for whatever reason, be-cause that voice was part of you for so long, you need something to replace it. You don't really love me, you just want me to tell you what to do."

"Then you don't love me."

"I thought I loved you for a time, but I found out that what we shared wasn't love, but need. We needed each other, because we had nothing else, no one else in the world to trust. That isn't love, Kathy."

She stared straight out through the windshield, and then, to his surprise, she nodded.

"I want you to say you'll do one more thing for me."

He started to speak but she put a finger on his lips, silencing him.

"It's a simple thing," she said. "Do it because I ask you. I want you to meet me in Ranier Park tomorrow, at five o'clock.

He studied her a moment, trying to read her face, and then he said, "All right."

It was a raw March day, spring only a week away but wet snow was falling. It was already dark. Corrie's work boots made black footprints in the slushy mixture as he entered the park, hands deep in his parka's pockets, baseball cap getting wet on his head.

He vaguely heard the slam of a car door and saw a figure approaching the entrance behind him but moved on, putting his head down.

The wind was sharp, picking up. The ice cut like tiny white knives against his face. He wished he had worn a woolen coat, a cap. His boots made wet, slurpy sounds as he walked to the picnic area.

He stopped. Wind whistled high above in the trees; some ice had coated the higher branches and it tinkled like glass. There was no moon behind the clouds, and a *thin, chilled fog pooled along the ground like snakes of smoke.*

"Kathy?" he called out.

He heard something behind him, and turned, but no one was there.

He trudged on, past the picnic area, into the woods.

Again he heard a sound behind him, and abruptly stopped. The sound, like an echo, halted a half-second later. "Kathy?" he called again.

The wind howled, driving wet snow and hail at his unprotected face.

He turned and made a horn of his hands, shouting into the woods: "Kathy!"

There were only the sounds of the storm, and he pushed on.

He came abruptly to the small clearing where they had made love, and nearly tripped over a heavy rock that had obviously been moved there. Under it was a rope that snaked loosely along the ground and up the trunk of a huge nearby pine tree and next to it was a soaked manila envelope.

He picked the envelope up and angled it toward the faint light from the gray glowing sky.

OPEN ME, it read.

He ripped it open and drew out a single sheet of paper, dotted with wet spots. A smudged single line of handwriting said: PULL THE ROPE.

Becoming angry at the game, he picked up the rope and took two steps back until it went taut. Then he gave it a yank—

He heard a gasp, and something crashed down

through the branches of the pine and came up short five feet off the ground.

It was Kathy Marks, hands bound in front of her, rope around her neck leading up into the pine tree.

"Kathy!" Corrie shouted, dropping the rope, but it had no effect on Kathy, who was struggling for breath, her body swinging to and fro—

"Don't move!" a voice shouted behind Corrie.

He turned around, confused, his hands held out.

A man was standing with his eye aimed down the barrel of a gun at Corrie.

"But—"

"Shut up and get on the ground!"

A second man stepped out of the trees into the clearing.

"Bill, let him get the girl down."

The first man continued to aim at Corrie. "I saw him yank the rope! He's killing her!"

The second voice, more reasonable, said to Corrie, "Son, hoist her up on your shoulders. I'll help you in a minute, after I give a life lesson to this police officer."

"But I saw—!" the first man shouted. The second man was aiming at the first.

"If you make a move to shoot him, I'll have to shoot you, Bill. Lower your gun."

Corrie had taken a tentative step toward the tree; the man named Bill followed him with his gun.

"Go on, son," the second man said to him. "Before it's too late."

Corrie took another step toward the thrashing figure of Kathy Marks, then ran the remaining steps and lifted her up.

A shot rang out, and suddenly the rope collapsed, and Kathy Marks fell onto Corrie, who broke her fall. Then she was on the ground, and Corrie quickly loosened the rope from around her neck.

The second cop, fat and with a thoughtful yet kind face, stood over the two of them and tucked his gun away. "It's nice to see I can still shoot when I have to," he said.

Corrie looked up to see the first cop, gun hanging loosely at his side, looking down at the ground and breathing heavily.

"Don't worry about him, son, he'll be all right," the second cop said—

The banging was not part of the dream, but was very loud, and finally Corrie woke up. He gave a start, finding himself in his bed, not wet and cold with an unconscious Kathy Marks in his arms.

The banging continued.

He was too exhausted to move.

Hoarsely, and then forcefully, he shouted through the open door, "Come in!"

Ted Bright heard a muffled shout from within the quiet house, which was followed by a distinct call for him to come in. He tried the front door he had been banging on for five minutes and it was unlocked.

He pushed open the door, entering partial gloom. To his left was a dark first floor, but straight in front of him was a landing and a stairway leading up.

"Corrie Phaeder?" he called.

There was light upstairs, but there was no answer.

Then he heard a familiar sound issuing from upstairs: thunder, lightning and the crash of mighty waves.

"Jesus," Bright whispered.

He mounted the stairs and stood at the top of the landing; at the end of a short hallway was a room with its door open, bright light within.

He approached it, his heart hammering.

He stood in the doorway, expecting to be hit by a mighty wave of water.

The bedroom was filled with light and sound.

And in the center of the room, in the exact same position as his daughter had been earlier, was Corrie Phaeder, gasping for air, floundering and suspended in space.

Chapter Twenty-one

The doctor tried to gently bring up the NO SMOKING sign to Grant, but then gave up.

Already thinking lawsuit, Grant thought absently as he lit a second Kent from the ash of his first. He dropped the first on the waiting room floor and ground it out on the linoleum.

"Terrible accident," the doctor was saying. His name was Jones or James, something like that, and he was young and nervous and probably competent and rattled as hell. "Something like this happens once in ten thousand electroshock treatments. The shocks just stop the heart. It's very rare, but it happens. It's in the disclosure and release forms."

Grant's look made him stop talking. "I want to see her."

"Of course," the doctor said. He held a door open for Grant, then another door—the hated an-

tiseptic smell tickled Grant's nostrils, disappeared
when the third door closed behind them, replaced
by a new odor: burned meat. Grant wondered if
perhaps some intern or technician had wandered
away, forgotten . . .

Grant spied a small kitchen off to the right of
the hallway they were in, a stove, a hamburger
smoking in a frying pan, unattended.

A swinging door, and the air-conditioned, anti-
septic smell was back. She was on a flat gurney,
eyes closed, dressed in a white hospital gown.

Grant looked down at her—

She looked as peaceful as she ever had.

"She wanted to be cremated," Grant said; "I'll
call you with the arrangements."

Grant was sure of the relief in the voice: *No autopsy*, the young doctor was thinking.

"The Gannon Funeral Home people will be in
touch right after the autopsy."

He took a secret, sick pleasure in feeling the
other man stiffen.

Grant bent down and kissed Rose, closing his
eyes as he always had, ever since their first kiss.

*Good-bye, baby. I never stopped loving you. Not for a
minute.*

"Don't worry, asshole, I'm not going to sue
you," he said to the doctor on the way out.

They were holding Marvin Soames in the drunk
tank. Grant was mildly annoyed about that, until
he saw the condition the man was in.

Pell Simpson, who had accompanied Grant to the back reaches of the jail, remarked, "Hell, we almost sent him to the hospital—looked like alcohol poisoning. But then he puked and woke up for a while so we decided to keep him here for you."

"Thanks, Farmer."

The tall, thin detective hesitated. "Say, Bill . . ."

"I'm okay, Farmer. You gave me your condolences upstairs. I'll let you know about the arrangements. I'll be okay."

"Wouldn't you rather be home?"

Grant turned his tired eyes on his co-worker. He reached into his jacket pocket for a cigarette but then stopped; he couldn't get away with it here. "Pell, if I go home I'll go nuts. I won't be able to concentrate on anything, and the phone won't stop ringing. If I do it my own way, I'll be fine."

He found himself laying a hand on Farmer's arm, though he still didn't know the man very well. "If I need you I'll call you, podna."

Farmer's eyes widened slightly. "Riley Gates used to use that term."

"Still did, until yesterday." Grant nodded toward Marvin Soames, sleeping on the iron bunk in the cell, snoring slightly. "Leave me alone with this squirrel, will you?"

"Sure. Just be . . ." he nodded at the cold eye of the video camera mounted on the wall behind them; its wide-angle lens covered the drunk tank and the two holding cells, currently empty, next to it.

"Yeah, Big Brother. I won't lay a hand on him."

Farmer gave a thin, humorless smile. "I almost did myself. We found him with the knife he used, passed out on the floor of Riley's barn. Just doesn't seem possible that a souse like this could take out Riley Gates."

Grant was staring at the snoring man. "No, it doesn't."

Five minutes later Bill Grant was alone in the cell with Marvin Soames. There was a wooden stool in one corner, and he drew it close to the bed and sat regarding the drunk before he woke him up. Almost immediately, he moved the stool back a couple feet—Soames smelled to high heaven. One shoe was missing half its lace, tied at mid-point up its grommets; his trousers were filthy, his shirt tatters held together by air. One elbow on the flannel shirt was rubbed through, and it was buttoned wrong. Soames hadn't shaved in a while, and his last haircut was a distant memory.

Grant toed the sleeping man's thigh. "Marvin, wake up."

Soames snorted, put his hands out, then tried to roll over, still snoring every third or fourth breath.

Grant kicked him harder, moving it up to his ribs.

"Soames, get the hell awake."

The man's eyes snapped open, and he uncurled into a sitting position.

"Sam?"

"No, it's Grant. Time to talk."

The man's eyes looked through Grant, then slowly came to focus.

"Holy shit."

"I'd say that's what you're in, Marvin. Unholy shit, more like."

Soames was staring at him intently. "I know you . . ."

Grant nodded slightly. "I'm a friend of Riley Gates."

Soames nodded vigorously, up and down. "Knew it. How is Riley? You know, I get pissed sometimes when I think of Riley runnin' me in like he did those two times, but, hell, I guess he was just doin' his job. You, too." He looked around him. "What'd I do?"

"We're pretty sure you killed Riley Gates."

Soames's eyes grew wide as saucers. "No!"

Grant nodded. "You put a knife into him in his own pumpkin patch yesterday, Marvin."

Something strange happened then. Grant had grown accustomed to drunks over the years. They had peculiar thought processes born of a pickled brain. They could be very precise, but only on isolated matters. When they concentrated on one single thing, they were as good a witness as anyone. But that single thought existed in a vacuum. It was as if they were in a closed-in bubble and the rest of the world, literally, did not exist.

Marvin's face went through a series of contortions, as if he were flipping through various isolated memories. It was like watching a pinball hit different lighted targets. And then he seemed to hit the jackpot.

His face collapsed. He stared down at his hands as if everything he owned was there.

"Oh Lord God," he said.

"Marvin?" Grant urged. "Did you kill Riley Gates?"

"These hands killed him," Soames said, in a low, sure voice. "But it was Sam did the killing."

"Sam?"

Marvin nodded, and his eyes met Grant's. The fear and confusion in the them was startling. "Man in a cape. Not much of him there, mind you. Brings me things, wine and such. We talk. Never asked me to do anything until yesterday. Asked me not to tell—"

As if a switch had been hammered off, he shut up.

"Marvin?"

"Can I have a drink, Mr. Grant?" His voice sounded like a child who had done a bad thing.

"That I can't do, Marvin. But we can get you fixed up pretty good if you tell me—"

"You have to do it anyway—it's the law," Soames said. He was suddenly crafty. "I know the law. You'll dry me out and stand me up. I can take it. Took it when Riley Gates hauled me in those two times. I'll take it now."

Grant fought to control his voice. "Who's Sam, Marvin?"

174

"What?" Soames had moved off into another bubble of memory.

"Tell me who Sam is and I'll see about getting you a bottle."

"White zin?"

"Anything you want."

Again, Soames's face was a map of fighting bits of memory. He was staring at one of the blank walls.

"Man in a cape. No man there, really. Brings me white zin most every day."

"*I'll* bring you white zin," Grant said.

"Behind the tree? Thanks, Samhain . . ."

Something went ice cold in Grant. He glanced out through the bars of the drunk tank to make sure the red light was on under the all-seeing video eye. "What did you say, Marvin?"

"White zin would be nice. Good lunch wine. Do whatever you ask."

His head whipped around and he glared intently at Grant. "You're not Sam! Get out! Lemme be!"

He lay back down on the hard bunk and curled away from Grant.

In another few moments he was snoring again, dead asleep.

Grant got up, pushed the stool back against the wall, and let himself out of the drunk tank.

When he checked the tape from the interview, Soames had said everything Grant thought he'd said.

Everything.

Chapter Twenty-two

"One week."

The wisp of smoke stood atop what had once been a mountain of sorts. Now it was a blackened pile of soot. The sky overhead, coal black, filled with a thick fog of dust, had been eaten half away; in the scant moments when the roiling clouds parted there was a ragged line separating something from nothing that looked as if it had been made by bite marks.

In a way it had.

The thin wisp of smoke repeated its mantra: "One week." Beside it was a shape that resembled a cardboard cutout, and another that looked like a patch of red silk, floating off the ground like a manta ray.

"One week and the Dark One will have made it to the Untouched Lands," the ray said, in a voice like air leaking from a tire.

The cardboard cutout said, "We'll do our best to fight them off—"

As they watched, there was a booming sound like an immense tearing of fabric and another portion of the sky disappeared, leaving a fresh ragged bite mark.

The ground beneath them trembled.

The wisp of smoke said, "The three helpers have done their job well. But I'm afraid the girl is being brought along too quickly."

"It can't be helped. There's no time—"

"This is true. Have the three withdrawn, now?"

"Yes, there are other things at work. More elaborate things. In a few days she will be on a level with the young man."

"That is good, because both of them must be ready by Halloween."

"They will be."

"You still think the girl is our best hope?"

The cardboard cutout was silent for a moment. "Yes. The young man is . . . unstable. Perhaps untrustworthy."

All three of them watched the ragged sky being eaten, listened to the booming of distant destruction.

"One week," the wisp of smoke whispered.

Chapter Twenty-three

"Hello, again."

Corrie jumped, and turned around to see John standing behind him. The pumpkin man's head glowed with an eerie, flickering light as if a candle within were being buffeted by wind. John reached out and touched him on the shoulder.

"Visiting?" John inquired.

"Yes . . ." Corrie said vaguely. He couldn't quite remember how he had gotten here. He remembered leaving the house, which had been lit up from within as if fires burned in every window; there had been the sounds of a volcano eruption, and he thought he had ridden down the stairs on a river of lava—

He looked at his hands—they were burned as if—

He remembered passing houses decorated for Halloween: uncarved pumpkins on porches, or-

179

ange lights in strings across gutters, cutouts in windows. One of the cutouts, a black cat, turned its fierce yellow eyes on him and hissed as he went by. Another, of a cutout jointed skeleton, had looked at him and then begun to climb out of the window and follow him. When he blinked and looked at it, it was just a cutout in a window again. It must have been late; house lights were off and the distant sounds of barking dogs and a lonely, faraway train whistle were all he heard. He passed through town, quiet in the late hour, the orange stripe down Main Street still looking fresh after the Pumpkin Days Festival, the tents in Rainer Park gone. He felt like a visitor from another planet. He heard his own footsteps, looked down to see holes opening in the street in front of him, which he avoided, weaving like a drunk. When he looked back the holes were gone. He passed a bar, still open, and crossed the street so he wouldn't be seen.

The other side of town, past the municipal building holding the court and town government, a few restaurants and Mom and Pop stores, and then he was out of town again. Two rows of sleeping houses, and then a lonely country road lined with denuded trees. Leaves fell like snow. He broke out into a clearing, the moon overhead staring balefully down at him, then suddenly resolving into a deformed face, the mouth opening wide in a howl:

"Corrie . . ."

He looked away, looked back, and the moon was

growing, flying down at him out of the heaven, widening, filling the sky—

He closed his eyes and then opened them once more.

The moon was as it should be, hanging serenely in the sky.

Then the gate to the cemetery, creaking open, back and forth, back and forth on its rusty hinges . . .

"I can't tell the difference between reality and . . . the other anymore," he said, blinking at John. "I've been watching for you; you haven't been in the cornfield . . ."

"I've been busy elsewhere," John remarked. "And as for . . ." He reached out a cornstalk hand, touched Corrie's palm. "As I said, it will only get worse. For you, two worlds are merging. Mine is becoming more real to you. Be aware that the dead in your world appear differently than they do in mine. In my world they will look . . . extremely strange to you. Not like ghosts or goblins or the other manifestations of the next life you're used to. Not like me. Your eyes will perceive them in . . . odd ways."

"Like the shapes Reggie and I have been seeing in our dreams?"

"Yes."

"The girl, Reggie, her father came to see me the other night, he doesn't understand . . ."

John was silent; the light burned bright behind

181

his eyes. "It will be very hard for her. Her parents will try to stop you. If you can't make them understand, you must at least protect her."

There was a long silence. "She may be very important in the end, Corrie."

"What do you mean?"

"That's not something I should talk about now."

A flare of anger shot through Corrie. "You're doing to her what you did to me! After everything you've done to me, the horrors you've put me through, you have to do it to a little girl too?"

John's voice was gentle. "I'm sorry, Corrie, but it's necessary . . ."

"Let her go! Let her have her life back! It's too late for me, I've been in a nightmare since I was seven, but *let her go!*"

John looked at the ground. "We can't do that. *I* can't do that. We just don't know . . ."

"Jesus. Jesus . . ."

Corrie blinked, turned around. He was shaking. The gravestone he had been staring at stared back at him mutely: GRACE PHAEDER, it read on the dull gray surface.

Corrie's voice caught in his throat. "I . . . came to tell her I'm sorry."

Again John put a hand on him, removed it.

"I'll see you again soon. On Halloween. Be strong until then."

A rustling sound began in a whisper, quickly grew to a hiss and then a moan.

"What—"

Corrie turned around, but John had vanished.

The gravestones around him flared with light. In front of each stone, a line of smoke rose screaming, corkscrewing out of the ground and resolving into a human shape—man, woman, child—and then settling on the ground. Their movements were stiff, disjointed, as if they were unused to Corrie's world.

His mother's grave was silent; no ghost rose.

The ghosts turned their hollow eyes on him, and each held a hand out—

"Corrrriieeeeee," one of them said, and then the others joined in chorus:

"Corrrrrrrrrrieeeeeeeee . . ."

Corrie backed away from his mother's burial spot, holding his hands out to ward off the spirits who walked without touching the ground.

"Corrrrriieeeee . . ."

He turned and ran, stumbling to the cemetery gate and then turning around.

The ghosts were spiraling back down into their graves, hisses of blue-white vapor.

"I'm sorry . . ." Corrie whispered, looking at his mother's silent grave.

He ran back to his house, which waited for him, opening the door wide and then closing it behind him with finality.

Chapter Twenty-four

After the ceremony for Rose, which, as Grant wanted, was a small one, and the one for Riley, which was even smaller, with just a few retired cops, and Captain Farrow conspicuously absent, Grant drove to the library. He hoped the librarian would be off that day, but she was working, so there was nothing to do but talk to her.

"Hello, Ms. Marks. Do you remember me?"

She stared at him a moment. "Detective . . . Grant?"

"That's right."

She looked much older than the last time he had seen her. Older, and used up. She looked more than tired; she reminded him of Rose, when the depression had first taken over. Rose would sit for hours, staring at the television but not watching it; when he talked to her she would listen, but not hear.

"Can I help you with something, detective?"

"Actually, yes. I'm looking for a book called"—he consulted his open notebook—"*Occult Practices in Orangefield and Chicawa County, New York, 1668–1940.*"

A brief flicker of interest sparked on her face. She frowned. "That's in the Local History section, upstairs. It's a restricted book, but of course you can borrow it."

"Thanks."

He mounted the spiral staircase behind the librarian station, watching Kathy Marks as he went up. Her gaze had gone blank again.

He quickly located the Local History section, and the book he wanted. Sure enough, it was by Thomas R. Reynolds. His eyes browsed over a few other RESTRICTED titles: *A Short History of Halloween, An Occult History of Orangefield* by D.A. Withers—the last he paged through and then decided to take as well.

As he descended the staircase to the main floor, he made a decision.

"Ms. Marks, can I speak with you for a moment?"

She looked up at him, seemed to stare through him. "Of course."

Like an automaton, she processed his two books and gave them back to him. "There's a conference room in the back we can use," she said. After calling over one of the young assistants who worked with her to man the desk, she led him there, closing the door behind them.

She sat down on one side of a table, and Grant sat down on the other.

"This isn't official business or anything," Grant said, making sure that his voice sounded official enough to get her attention. He opened his notebook and put it on the table in front of him, also to get her attention.

She looked at the notebook.

Grant said, "I just wanted to ask you if you're all right."

Another flicker of interest. "Personally? I hardly think my personal life—"

Grant held up a hand. "I'm not trying to meddle. But I know a little bit about depression—my late wife was a victim—and, frankly, you show all the symptoms."

As expected, she reddened with indignation. "Detective—"

"It's nothing to be ashamed of. I know an excellent man here in Orangefield who can help you." He scribbled a name down on an empty sheet of notebook paper, tore it out and slid it over to her. "I'm not telling you this as a cop. Believe me, I'm just trying to help."

He got up and looked down at her—she looked as if she wanted to cry or scream or crawl deeper into her shell. On a whim he took out one of his cards and slid that over to her, too. "If you ever need someone to talk to, call me. I've been through it—all of it—with my wife. My home phone and cell are on there, too."

He left her there, wondering if he had done the right thing.

At home, he cleared a spot on the kitchen table and opened the Reynolds volume. The first chapters were fascinating, covering Salem witch trial-like occurrences in the Orangefield area in the late 17th century—Grant hadn't known that a total of fourteen persons had been executed by hanging or stoning for witchcraft. Reynolds's contention was that the executions here did not attain the notoriety of the Salem trials because no burnings at the stake were involved. Much of the rest of the book covered similar events from colonial times through the early 1900s, the standard 'strange happening' cases, unsolved mysteries, that sort of thing.

Then Grant hit the last chapter, titled THE PUMPKINFIELD ERA AND THE BEGINNING OF 'SAMHAIN SIGHTINGS,' and his interest picked up. He got a bottle of Dewars from the liquor cabinet and poured himself a stiff drink, then sat down to study Reynolds's research.

Under the chapter title was a picture of the first pumpkin field in Orangefield. Grant already knew that the town's name had been briefly changed to Pumpkinfield during the Depression.

There followed a discussion of "Samhain sightings," or "Sam sightings," which began around 1941. Apparently there was another rash of sightings in 1952, but that was covered in the second volume, which Grant had not been allowed to see. There were unsolved murders involved. Samhain was usually described as a cloaked figure who often appeared in pumpkin patches. The book ended abruptly. Grant was unsatisfied.

He turned to *An Occult History of Orangefield* by D.A. Withers, but discovered to his dismay that the book covered mainly colonial times. It had been written in 1953.

Damn.

Grant poured himself another Dewars and sat staring at the cover of the Reynolds book.

He had another scotch. And then another.

He decided he wanted to see the second volume.

Badly.

He took out his notebook and flipped to the page with the Reynolds's telephone number on it.

There was the slightest of movements behind him, and then a voice said: "Perhaps I can help."

Grant was not a jumpy man, but he nearly leapt out of his chair, spilling his drink as he spun around. His hand was already to his shoulder holster, drawing his 9mm as he turned.

The kitchen door was open. In the opening floated what looked like a black cloak surrounding an amorphous figure. Grant couldn't quite grasp the features; they were insubstantial, here and then gone, as if illuminated by a flickering light bulb. The face was pale gray, the eyes hooded, the mouth a cruel red slash.

Grant had his gun out, trying to point it.

"It will make a lot of noise, and accomplish nothing," the figure said. The voice was rich, and not without a touch of humor. "Think about all the paperwork."

"You're Samhain," Grant managed to get out.

"Yes. You could read about me in Volume Two of that fool Reynolds's work, but I'll save you the trouble. Volume Two is gone anyway, and young Reynolds and his mother with it. I asked them politely to leave, though I have a feeling the boy may be back someday. He's a lot stronger than his father."

The cloak flapped, the face became more starkly lit for a moment. A shiver passed through Grant.

"There are things I can do, Detective Grant, and things I cannot do," Samhain said. "Certain . . . humans, of a weaker mind, can be handled. Someone like you, on the other hand, would be impossible to influence directly.

"But there's always the indirect approach. Your wife, for instance. Her doctor, or the attendant he left her care to, I should say, could be handled."

"You murdered her . . ."

"Let's just say I was able to put certain wheels in motion, which turned the way I wanted them to. Sometimes I can control some parts of nature: insects and, sometimes, animals. You'll remember the first time we rubbed shoulders, Detective Grant. The hornets at Peter Kerlan's house. And later at the bee keeper's. Marvin Soames has a weak mind, also. Do you see a pattern?"

"Riley Gates, Fred Willims, Charlie Morton, Rose . . ."

"Ah, ever the good detective. I'm glad you remember the district attorney, who was susceptible to a hornet sting. He was easy—as most lawyers are. I'm trying to control you indirectly, my friend. Through persuasion. We all work for someone. The someone I work for wants the wheels I've put into motion to continue to turn. My job is to insure that happens. Riley Gates was a potential problem, which was taken care of indirectly. The same could happen to you."

The red slash of a mouth became very solid: a hard smile, sharp as a scythe.

"I would like you to stay away from Corrie Phaeder. For a short while, I hoped you would take care of him for me, but that didn't happen. He didn't kill his mother, by the way. Just as Riley Gates told you."

Grant was staring at him. "Are you really . . . ?"

The red sickle smile widened. "The 'Lord of Death'? Something like that. But my subjects are unhappy, these days. Usually, I would have certain of them to assist me but these days the pickings are, shall we say, slim.

"The one I work for, though, is far worse than I am. I have always been interested in your species, in a clinical sort of way. My own master entertains no such foibles."

Suddenly the cloak was in the kitchen with Grant, flapping and moving directly in front of

191

him. Grant felt a coldness unlike any he had ever felt.

The eyes, which were emptiness, the opposite of light, bored into him. When Samhain opened his mouth again Grant felt an ice-blue freeze in the words. "The one I serve is worse than death, Detective. He is the opposite of life. When he drives through my domain into this one, he will obliterate every atom of every living thing on this world. He detests life. And I serve him because I must."

For a moment the voice became almost bitter: "Because I must. For me, it will be something of a rest I suppose . . ."

The cloak, the face, came even closer. The words were even colder, like being in the back of a freezer with the door locked in front of you. "Do nothing. Stay away from Corrie Phaeder. Watch Marvin Soames, if you like. With him, I will show you what I can do. One other, also, if you persist.

"Do nothing, Detective."

The cloak, the face, the unfathomable cold, were gone in a finger snap.

Grant looked at the kitchen door, which was closed.

He slowly turned back to the table.

The Dewars bottle was nearly empty, the spilled liquor vanished, fresh ice in the glass.

The books he had borrowed from the library were burned, a pile of ashes.

Chapter Twenty-five

To Gina, the world was now like a roller-coaster.

Sometimes she saw Mr. Phaeder in her dreams. Her dreams were the only part of her life that was real, now. When she saw Mr. Phaeder he was painting his porch, or pulling weeds, or fixing the door on his shed. In her dreams Mom and Dad took her to buy shoes, or to the video store, or they all went to lunch.

Awake, she was in wonderland. The playmates were gone, but Mr. Phaeder had started to appear in wonderland, too. It was as if, awake, they were having the same dreams, the same adventures. They would be in a plane, sometimes with Mr. Phaeder piloting and sometimes Gina, and the plane would fly high over a dark landscape without trees or rivers or houses. Sometimes strange figures would move below, but they could never get a good look at them and the plane wouldn't fly lower. Sometimes they were in a balloon or a blimp, but always they would be too high to see anything but the dark landscape and the strange moving shapes.

Lately, she and Mr. Phaeder had been able to talk a little during these adventures, but never for long, as if someone had told them to hush.

Mr. Phaeder didn't look too good, and Gina wondered how she looked herself. Mr. Phaeder had bruises all over his arms and his face, and his hair had gotten thinner, and turned gray; when Gina tried to look at her own arms she found that she could not look directly at herself, as if her sight slid off her body and made her look a little to the side. But she didn't feel too bad, and ate some of the food that Mom left for her in her room.

She hadn't left her room in a long time, as far as she knew.

She remembered two trips, one to the doctor and one over a bridge, but they were at least a week ago, probably longer, and she remembered a lot of yelling in the car after they went through the bridge toll and then Dad turned around and they came back. After that she stayed in her room. It was just about then that wonderland had started for real, with only a little sleeping each day, which let her remember things like Mom and Dad buying groceries, or Dad mowing the lawn. Even these brief reality dreams were getting shorter, as wonderland began to take over.

That's what Mr. Phaeder had told her during

one of their short conversations while they were in the blimp: "Reggie, soon it will be Halloween, and then we're going on a trip."

Gina wondered if they were going to wonderland, or somewhere even stranger.

Gina remembered Halloween—she vaguely recalled that she was going to dress up like a princess this year. Or was that last year? Even the reality dreams were getting mixed up lately, but she had no doubt that, this year, Halloween would be an event.

Later, when she and Mr. Phaeder were in a helicopter, he had assured her that it certainly would, though he wasn't smiling when he said it.

Right now Gina was in a balloon alone—or rather she was in a chair to which hundreds of party balloons, red, green, blue, yellow, filled with helium were attached, and she was floating above the dark landscape. Off in the distance she saw another figure in a chair supported by twice as many balloons, and she imagined that must be Mr. Phaeder. They were slowly drifting toward each other.

Somewhere out of wonderland, Gina heard a door open and close, and then her mother crying. It must be time for lunch or dinner. Very faintly, she thought she felt her mother's hands touch her, but it was more like someone breathing on your skin than grabbing you. Then the weeping stopped and the door was opened and closed again.

Mr. Phaeder was within hailing distance now, and Gina waved to him.

"Hello, Reggie!" he called, making a cup of his hands.

Gina tried to yell back at him, but nothing came out of her mouth.

Mr. Phaeder pointed down, and Gina looked to see that the landscape below had changed. Or maybe it had just gotten closer, because she could see the strange figures a little more clearly. There were cubes and wheels that rolled along by themselves, and wriggly strings that looked like snakes and balls of fluff like cotton. They were all moving in the same direction, and now Mr. Phaeder was yelling at her again to get her attention and pointing to the horizon in the direction in which all the strange shapes were moving.

Gina looked that way, and saw a brightening, and that the ground wasn't so dark down there. It seemed crowded with figures, thousands and thousands of roiling weird shapes. And there was a wide tall building made of stone. Then Mr. Phaeder was pointing the other way, and Gina saw that the other horizon was as black as night and that there was a ragged tear across the sky which got bigger as she watched it. There were rumbling sounds like the ones she had heard in her room, and hoots and whistles and faraway crashes.

Mr. Phaeder was moving away from her again, rising. He was waving his hands excitedly. Gina saw that she was sinking as Mr. Phaeder rose, making it seem like she was moving twice as fast.

The ground was rushing up at her.

There was a circle of strange shapes—a long sliver of puffy smoke, a flat figure that looked like a Halloween cutout, and some others, looking up at her and reaching out arms (if they had them) to break her fall or to help her down. But she stopped in midair just out of their reach.

There was much noise, a loud ripping sound and crashes like waves slamming into a sandy beach, and the figures themselves made sounds, other ones she had heard in her room.

For a second it looked like she was going to fall into their arms. The cardboard cutout leaped up, and nearly touched her foot, but missed. He fell back down with a crackly sound like crumpled cellophane.

But she stayed where she was, and then was yanked up a little higher, out of their reach. And Mr. Phaeder suddenly dropped down out of the sky, some of his balloons popped but there were still enough to keep him from falling. He came to a stop just next to Gina, and his mouth was working, but no words came out.

Then suddenly, as if someone had pushed a mute button off on a radio which was on but you couldn't hear, his words came booming out of his mouth. He was very excited, and looked very afraid.

It occurred to Gina that perhaps she should be very afraid, too.

"Tomorrow is Halloween," he said.

Chapter Twenty-six

Marvin Soames was mightily pissed off.

Not only that: he was thirsty. Real thirsty. Thirsty as he'd ever been.

And now they went and stuck him in the basement.

The drunk tank had been fine; the holding cell they'd put him in after that had been fine, too. At least they'd both been on the first floor. There had been the occasional other guest of the town to hob-nob with—briefly, before they moved him to the holding cell, he'd shared the drunk tank with Jelly Gomez and Brenda Whats-her-name, drinking buddies from way back. He hadn't seen Jelly in two years, and Brenda didn't look so good, either. Of course they both said the same thing about him, and gave him big eyes.

"You really a *cop killer*, Marvin?" Jelly had said in disbelief.

"That's what they tell me," Marvin had answered, and for a moment he felt important, because Jelly and Brenda moved to the other side of the cell, like they were afraid of him. Then he felt lonely.

But not as lonely as when that crazy bastard Grant came barging in and had him moved to the basement. That was two days ago. Grant didn't look so good himself these days; had that bender look to him that Marvin knew so well, a little flaked around the edges, eyes dull and too alert at the same time. 'Course he'd just lost his wife, which must be tough, and Marvin had told him that, which didn't stop Grant from having him moved to the cellar.

"For your own protection," Grant had said, when asked.

"From who?" Marvin asked. "How 'bout a drink?"

When he thought about who, he had a couple of possibilities, neither of which he was comfortable with.

Here came one of them now.

That fat sonovabitch Prohman was waddling toward him with a tray in his paws. Soames liked him about as much as he enjoyed hemorrhoids. He'd heard stories about Prohman, from guys like Jelly and Fritz Breamer, about years ago when Prohman had been a beat cop. Not so fat then, but the story was he liked to use the stick. Soames had always avoided him like the plague.

"Mr. Soames, dinner time!" Prohman announced, sliding the tray under the bars—clumsy bastard didn't even notice that he'd knocked the soda over doing it. Now the chips and sandwich were soaked.

Marvin grunted.

"What's the matter, Mr. Soames—ain't hungry?"

Prohman's tone had altered subtly: lower, a hint of meanness.

Marvin grunted again, looking at the soaked tray.

When he looked up, Prohman was unlocking the door. His piggy eyes were bright and Marvin's attention was drawn to the billy club in the fat cop's hand.

Prohman took a step in—and then froze as Detective Grant appeared at the bottom of the basement steps.

"Chip, what the hell are you doing?" Grant growled.

Prohman immediately shoved the billy down into the front of his pants and bent down to the tray.

"Goddam cop-killing drunk messed up his dinner," Prohman stammered, picking up the tray and turning around to face Grant.

The detective studied him closely. "Take the tray upstairs and get him another one."

Prohman tried to smile but lost it.

"And get that stick out of your pants," Grant added. "Makes you look like you've got something going on down there."

As the fat sergeant passed Grant the detective said, "You'll be on the desk for the rest of your life."

Prohman hurried away and stomped up the stairs.

Grant slowly swung the cell door closed and locked it from the outside. He stared in at Soames.

"How you doing, Marvin? We're going to move you tomorrow to the state prison."

Marvin looked at the floor. The need and jitters were back. "Could use a drink."

"Couldn't we all. You know it'll pass."

Soames harrumphed. "Hasn't ever."

"How long you been like this?" the detective asked.

Marvin shrugged. "Long time, I guess. Troubles, you know."

"When did you first meet Samhain?"

Marvin was studying his hands, which were moving one over the other in front of him. "While ago. Fritz Breamer and some of the others, they made me move on. Can't blame them much, I wasn't bringing in much in the way of trade. Used to be you could get enough empties to bring to the mart for a bottle, but all the younger guys and the kids seem to snap them up 'fore I got to 'em. Don't know . . ." He studied his hands, forgot Grant's question.

"What did Samhain say to you, Marvin?"

Soames's attention focused on the tone in

Grant's voice. He looked up to see the detective's tired eyes intently on him.

"Say, Detective, how 'bout we share a drink along with our troubles? I surely am sorry about your wife. I know you can get a bottle if you want."

"Not now, Marvin. What about Samhain?"

Marvin shrugged. "He just sort of came to me one day. I was pretty down and out and then, boom, there's a bottle of zin just waiting for me when I wake up. And he talked to me, first in my head and then I saw the cloak."

"When was that?"

Another shrug. "Don't know. A year, maybe more." He seemed trying to concentrate. "One winter, two winters."

"And he took care of you all that time?"

"Bottle every day." He smiled, looking down at his moving hands again. "Asked him for two on Christmas, but he said that wouldn't be appropriate."

"And what was your end of the bargain?"

"Nothing much. Sort of like that undertaker, you know."

"I don't get it, Marvin."

Soames showed impatience. "That undertaker. In that movie. When the Godfather does him a favor, and says he may ask him for one later. And then later comes when his son gets shot up, and he asks the undertaker to make him look good again. Sure about that drink, Detective?"

"Sorry, Marvin. Like I said, we'll be sending you to the state prison tomorrow morning."

"Think it will help me?"

"What?"

"What I did to Riley Gates and all. I still say he wasn't a bad guy. Just did what he had to. But I was the undertaker. Think if I explain to them that Samhain was the Godfather, it'll help me?"

"It might. Good-night, Marvin."

There was a series of loud snapping bangs somewhere far off, muffled by the basement walls.

"What's that?" Marvin asked.

"Just firecrackers. Pre-Halloween fun. There's a kid named Lenny who sets them off in front of the station every year the night before Halloween. He'll be in a cell upstairs in fifteen minutes."

Chip Prohman clumped back down the stairs holding a tray with a new dinner on it.

"Make sure he eats it," Grant ordered. "And if you open that cell I'll know."

Grant glared at the fat man and went upstairs.

Prohman looked after him and said something under his breath.

"I didn't hear that, but I know what it was," Grant called back.

More firecrackers. At least that's what it sounded like. Or someone snapping his fingers.

Marvin woke up in darkness. There was a rustling sound, and he thought the fat cop might be in the cell. He called out. But there was only a snoring sound.

A flapping rustle, and Samhain appeared.

He rose out of the darkness like a lamp coming out of fog. His cape moved, outlined at the edges with light, and his face was like a glowing gray balloon with black holes for eyes and a mouth like a knife blade edged with blood. Marvin had never noticed just how frightening he looked.

"Are you thirsty, Marvin?"

"I'll say," Soames answered carefully.

The weird red mouth opened and a chuckle came out. "Good. I brought you a bottle."

Out in the darkness, the snoring turned into a snort.

"What about the fat cop?" Marvin whispered.

Samhain said, "He'll sleep through this party."

The cape moved aside, and there was a bottle there, label turned toward Samhain. The cork had already been removed.

"White zin?" Marvin asked expectantly.

"Something better. A celebration. You deserve it."

Hungrily, Marvin reached out and turned the bottle around.

"Chateau . . ." he puzzled.

"It's French champagne. Better than Dom Perignon. As I said, a celebration."

"Of what?"

"Of your final task for me. You helped me once,

205

and did very well, and now you'll do one more thing that I ask."

"Anything you want, Godfather," Marvin assured him, lifting the bottle to his lips. "Hey, this is good! And it tickles!"

"Those are the bubbles. Enjoy it, Marvin."

Soames guzzled the champagne, tittered as the carbonation ran down his cheeks. "Better than Cold Duck. Fritz had a bottle of Tattingers one New Year's Eve, we took it from a college kid who passed out—"

He continued to guzzle, holding the bottle with both hands. "And this has a *kick*!"

"I should say so, Marvin. It's very good champagne."

"Whoa," Soames exclaimed, holding the bottle out to examine it. He shook it. There was a little left. "Haven't had a fast kick like this in a while."

Samhain waited patiently while Marvin finished the champagne.

"Now what?" Marvin asked. His sight was a little skewed. He stared at the swirling cloak, hoping that perhaps a second bottle would appear. When he looked at Samhain's face it didn't look quite so horrible now, the sharp edges blurred, the smiling mouth more friendly.

"Any chance—"

"I think that bottle was sufficient. Now I'd like you to perform that task for me."

"Yeah? What's that?"

Samhain smiled. "Have you ever heard of Renfield, Marvin?"

Soames pretended to think, because that's what Samhain seemed to want. Finally he said, "Never been there."

"It isn't a place. It's a person. Renfield was a character in a book called *Dracula*. Pity you never read it."

"Read a good porno once—sure you don't have a second bottle?"

"We won't need it. Here's what I want you to do, Marvin . . ."

Grant came in to the station on Halloween morning and found Chip Prohman asleep on a makeshift cot in the basement. In the gloom, and from where Grant stood some twenty feet from it, it looked as though Marvin Soames's cell was empty.

He pushed Prohman awake. "Those marshals come early?"

"Whu—?" the fat sergeant said, yawning himself into a sitting position.

"How long have you been asleep, Chip?"

"Don't know, 'xactly. What time is it?"

"It's after eight A.M."

"Wow. We gotta get Soames ready to go."

"He's still here?"

"Yeah, I—"

Grant pushed his way past Prohman and went to the cell. He put his hands on the bars, peering in—

"What the—"

His hands were slick with something; as he turned his palms to the weak light leaking in from the basement doorway he saw that they were colored red—

"Holy God in heaven."

Prohman had roused himself by now, and was ambling toward him.

"Hey, what—"

"Get the hell away, Chip. Just go upstairs."

Prohman continued forward, his eyes goggling. "What's that on the floor—"

"I said go upstairs!"

"Wha—oh shit—"

Prohman turned and heaved the meager contents of his stomach onto the concrete floor. The sour smell of bile mixed with coppery blood—

Grant slowly backed away from the cell, his hands held before him, trying to erase the sight of Marvin Soames, his body flat on its back in the middle of the cell, flayed open and empty from chest to groin, his own innards smeared over the floor in a messy line of handprints that led to the bars and up them, entrails wrapped like snakes and still dripping—

Chapter Twenty-seven

The world had changed for Corrie Phaeder. Black was white now, white black. Up, sometimes, was down, and left, often, was right. He knew he was being pushed into another place, and knew he was almost there.

He knew Reggie's parents had tried to stop him. At one point he felt blows from an unseen fist, and heard voices that sounded like the Brights' voices, but at the time he was on a train with his hand on the throttle, Reggie beside him happily pulling the whistle, and then the blows stopped and the sounds of the train overcame the screaming. He never saw their faces.

He hadn't been in the real world for days, but neither had he been in the one he was heading to. He saw John once, as in a dream, but he was on a carnival ride at the time, at an amusement park he had never been to (therefore it hadn't been one of his "real" dreams, which had stopped altogether), one with beautiful Christmas tree lights strung from poles and a ferris wheel lit up in white and green, and a carnival barker yelling, "Hurry, hurry, hurry!" though there were no other people around except for John, who was in another flying car of the red and chrome whirligig he rode. Reggie was with him then, too, and enjoyed the ride more than he did, wanting it to go on when the cars finally came to a stop. Corrie felt sick to his stomach and when he looked at the other car John had disappeared.

He and Reggie wandered the amusement park for a while, but the barker was gone and the lights began to dim and finally they found themselves in front of a tent that said FREAK SHOW on the front of it in bold letters on a bright yellow banner. The tent was red-and-white-striped, and there was an odd noise coming from inside it.

And then they found themselves inside the tent, and when Corrie looked back at the entrance the carnival barker was back, yelling to the empty darkness outside, "Hurry, hurry, hurry!"

Reggie tugged at his sleeve and he turned to look where she pointed.

"Run!" she said, and her voice came out low-pitched and strung out, as if it was a tape that had been slowed down.

There were wall to wall and ceiling to floor shelves against one wall of the tent, holding jars and boxes of all shapes and sizes. The cardboard box nearest to them, the size of a refrigerator, shook violently, as if something massive inside was trying to get out; next to it was a tiny box with a cover on it. From inside came a tiny mewling sound, like that from a miniature cat.

When Reggie reached out to take off the cover, the box disappeared in a puff of smoke.

"You're getting closer," someone said, the voice all pinched together, the opposite of how Reggie's voice had sounded, and Corrie looked up to see John at the opposite end of the tent, under an EXIT sign. The pumpkin man walked out of the exit and Corrie tried to follow, pulling Reggie after him, but he moved as if stuck in molasses.

Reggie tugged back, and they examined the jars, which were filled with a thick greenish liquid. Something floated in each, brushing along the front of each jar and just becoming visible for a moment before vanishing into the foggy liquid once more. There were miniature versions of the shapes they had seen from their balloon chairs: squares and cardboard cutouts and squiggles and puffs of smoke and others, like mushrooms and something that looked like a human ear with legs and arms, but no hands.

"Almost," Corrie heard, and once again there was a figure in the EXIT opening, but it was a tall curl of smoke, which suddenly flattened.

Then there was a sound like a bell tolling, very deep and slow, and the tent was gone and the amusement park was gone and they were on a plain that filled in with houses and trees like things being drawn as they watched, and the sun peeked up over the far horizon, and the sky became blue.

And then they were back in Orangefield, with real sky and real ground under their feet, standing outside Corrie's house, at the bottom of the porch steps, with the real sun coming up over the Sagett River in front of them, turning the distant cornfield golden-yellow and the closer, picked-clean pumpkin patches chocolate brown. The air felt cold as milk on the skin, and the sky was the deepest blue Corrie had ever seen. He smelled apples and allspice and the chilled smell of freshly carved pumpkins, and something else, the smell of the world rotting, of turned things from the ground and dead things. It was life and death all mixed up together.

And then John was between him and Reggie, with an arm around each of them, hugging them close, and Corrie felt the pumpkin man's gentle touch and heard his gentle, sad voice.

He said, "Later today you will leave this place, and come over. This is your last time here, the last strong hold your world will have on you. Some strange things will happen to you today, and then the crossover will come. The two worlds are finished intertwining; my world is ready for you. But you must take your leave of this one.

"Samhain will try to prevent you from leaving," John said. "Anything that happens today will be his doing. This is his only chance to stop you.

212

"Tonight you will come with me into my world, and we will try to stop Samhain. Until then, be careful."

His voice became very faint, and the pressure on Corrie's shoulder became weaker and weaker.

Down Sagett River Road, from the direction of Reggie's house, two figures were running toward them.

John had disappeared, but his voice lingered in the air like the Cheshire cat.

"Today is Halloween."

Chapter Twenty-eight

"Little early for me, Bill," Farmer said, studying his own dry glass.

Grant knocked back his second scotch, neat, and looked at his colleague. "Not for me. Not for today. Thanks for coming, Pell, even if you're not drinking. If I didn't tell someone, I would have busted a gut."

The bar was empty, and the booths too, except for the one they occupied. Pete Loughran, the eponymous bartender, stood putting washed glasses into their slots, idly watching the television, which had one of the mindless morning yak shows on.

Farmer was silent. Then he said, "You've been through an awful lot lately, Bill."

"And I didn't make any of this shit up. That . . . *thing* told me something would happen to Marvin

Soames, and something did. Someone smeared
him all over that cell . . ."

"And you don't think Marvin did that all by himself, without any encouragement? He was a cop
killer, Bill, on his way to a state prison where they
don't like cop killers. Hell, I'd believe Chip
Prohman did a number on him if I didn't know
Chip was such a fuck-up."

Grant was staring at him stonily. "You going to
play devil's advocate, Farmer, or are you going to
listen to me?"

Farmer reached for the Dewars bottle, but not
to pour himself a drink. He drew it toward his side
of the table and left it there. "I think maybe you
should stop drinking. It's eleven o'clock in the
morning and you're still on duty."

Grant leaned over and brought the bottle back
to his side of the table. He poured another three
fingers of scotch into his glass, watching it slosh
against the sides like water against a dam. "I can
drink by myself, Farmer, if you like."

Farmer tried to stare him down but failed. Finally he threw his hands up and drew the bottle
back toward him, tilting the neck until a couple of
fingers of amber fluid flowed into his own glass.

"Top o' the morning, and all that shit," he said.

Grant gave a sour smile. "That's more like it."

Farmer sighed. "Now tell me this again: you believe this Samhain is real, and that he made Marvin
Soames kill Riley Gates, then himself?"

"And Samhain's done plenty of other bad business in this town since 1940."

"1940 . . ." Farmer shook his head. "Hell, that was years before either of us was born."

"That's right."

Farmer shook his head. "Sorry, that's just not something I can go for. I remember the boogeyman stories when we were kids, the Sam sightings and all that, but to think this stuff was real . . ."

"Riley thought so, and now I know it is, too."

"And this Samhain threatened you?"

"Told me basically that he'd take care of Soames, and do some other things to stop me if he had to."

Farmer was still shaking his head.

"You've seen some dark stuff yourself, haven't you, Pell? Wasn't your mother—"

Pell's face turned to stone. "My stepfather killed my mother when I was a kid, and some local girl, too. Then he blew his own brains out. But I never claimed anyone named Samhain had anything to do with it."

"Hey, I'm sorry—" Grant began.

"Forget it," Pell said. His face softened. "I just don't talk about it, is all."

"But this stuff is real, Pell. And I don't know what to do about it. Riley knew it was real. Samhain committed those murders, he burned up those books on my kitchen table, and he told me to stay away from Corrie Phaeder."

217

Farmer looked surprised. "Corrie Phaeder? Jeez—is that what this is all about?"

Grant looked at his scotch, then drank some of it. "Not anymore. A couple of weeks ago I wanted that kid's nuts on a platter. Now I don't know . . ."

He looked up to see that Farmer had stood up, leaving his barely touched drink behind.

"What's the matter?" Grant asked, surprised.

Farmer looked down at him, the stony look back on his face. "I'm goin' back to work, Bill. What I think you should do is go home and have a couple more drinks, then fall asleep. I'll tell Captain Farrow you were shook up by what happened to Soames and needed a break. He may be a jerk but he'll buy that one."

Grant said, "Sit down, Pell."

Farmer shook his head. "Sorry, but I can't buy this supernatural crap. I think this is about that kid Corrie Phaeder, plain and simple. I suggest you wash it all out of your head. See you tomorrow."

Before Grant could answer, Farmer had turned around and was through the door of the bar, letting in an abrupt line of daylight. Then he was gone.

"Marital spat?" Loughran said from behind the bar, staring at Grant with a blank look on his face, drying rag in one hand, glass in the other.

Grant nodded. "Something like that, Pete."

"You ask me," the bartender answered, "It's this Halloween shit. Too much shit happens around Halloween now. I hate Halloween. Good for business but bad for the head."

Grant down the scotch left in his glass. "You ever heard of Samhain, Pete?"

The bartender grinned. "You mean Sam sightings, all that crap?"

Grant nodded.

"Sure. Remember once my brother Nat, he saw somethin' flapping around in the woods—turned out to be my Uncle Pete, who's I was named after, with a snootful and his jacket on backwards." He was still grinning as Grant shook his head.

"Thanks, Pete," Grant mumbled.

"Any time, Bill." The bartender turned back to his television and Grant turned back to his scotch. He started to pour another, which he knew would be the one to tip him from here to there, sobriety to numbness, but his hand on the bottle stopped and then he put the bottle back down on the table. He stared at it for a second, then took his hand off it and stood up.

"On my tab, will you, Pete?" he called as he walked to the front door.

The bartender said, "You bet," without taking his eyes from the television.

Something weird in the air. He had no idea what he would say to Phaeder when he got there—but if anyone knew about Samhain it must be him.

The hell with Samhain, and Captain Farrow, and anyone else telling him to stay away from the kid.

It was mid-morning, but already Halloween was in full swing in Orangefield. It was cool and warm at the same time—perfect late October weather. Grant had the window of the Taurus rolled down. A classroom full of what looked like third graders, decked out in their Halloween costumes, was marching along Main Street with their teacher, a petite blonde, leading them. They were probably heading for Erskine's Candy Store. Grant passed the establishment a moment later, and, sure enough, another class, this one generaled by a young brunette, was just leaving, each clutching a chocolate pumpkin lollipop. Every store along the street was dressed to the nines in Halloween finery: huge cutouts, some of them custom made, in windows—pumpkins and jointed skeletons and ghosts and black cats and witches. One picture window, in a drapery shop no less, had the entire front window blackened, with only finger-scratched letters forming HAPPY HALLOWEEN! breaking the startling mood. Grant could imagine how black the sponges they would use to remove that window scene would be the next day. Every light pole not only was bedecked in its plywood painted pumpkin at the apex, but also wrapped with black and orange tinsel like a barber pole. The barber himself (as opposed to the ten hair stylists spread around town) had replaced his own real pole for the season with a specially made one, striped white and orange.

And everywhere—*everywhere*—were carved pumpkins.

Even before he reached the residential area at the edge of town, the smell of fresh-scooped pumpkin filled his nostrils. There were pumpkins guarding every shop's doorway, and others that had been left overnight anonymously (a practice that had started a few years ago, and grown since) at bus stops, on public benches, next to post office drop boxes, and, especially, in front of the few establishments that refused, for one reason or another, usually crabbiness on the part of the owner, to participate in the town's biggest day. The most elaborately carved and largest were usually deposited here in the middle of the night—like Barney's Dry Cleaners. Barney wouldn't dare remove or destroy the pumpkin—this year, Grant saw, a tall oblong shape almost two feet in height and carved in the likeness, deliberate no doubt, of Barney's pinched face: eyes close together, downturned mouth in a sour pout. Then of course there were the costumed shopkeepers—the deli man at Carpy's who dressed like Mr. Spock from Star Trek once a year, the overweight yarn store owner who squeezed into her milkmaid outfit, the *very* overweight owner of Gund's Hardware, who fancied himself Felix the Cat, and who stood in front of his shop sweeping as Grant passed. There was a rip up the back of Gund's costume, which made him look anything but catlike.

Town Hall sported an orange and black banner with the mayor's name prominently displayed, welcoming all to Orangefield, THE PUMPKIN CAPITAL OF THE WORD. A couple of eggs already sported the mayor's name—many more would join them by tonight.

A few more shops, a couple of gas stations offering "Orange gas" (not really, but since one owner had offered it one year, increasing his business by ten percent, the two others had joined in, evening things out again) and then, almost abruptly, Grant had left the business district behind.

There were many more houses, mostly clustered in neat little developments with straight paved streets and tidy lawns, on the other side of Orangefield, the one closer to the main highway. On the west side of town were the older homes, the first-builts, the family mansions of the few town gentry (including the mayor, a succession of whose ancestors the town had loved to loathe for generations). The streets were broader here, the trees older and higher, closer together, more shielding of privacy. Some were gated. Many of the houses were Victorian in style. The newer ones stuck out like sore thumbs.

Grant liked it here, always had—it reminded him of a time when this was all there was to Orangefield, this cluster of old homes and a smaller place to live. When he had first visited it, when he was five, he had immediately fallen in love with it. The newer part of town, which had come later and could have been anywhere in America, had only detracted from Orangefield's charm, he thought.

He was soon through the old part of Orange-field, and turning onto Sagett River Road.

The sound of high rushing water already filled his ears.

Something alighted on his shoulder, and a voice said, "Can we talk?"

It was a gentle voice, almost a whisper, but still Grant had a violent reaction. His first thought was, *Samhain*. He yanked the wheel hard to the right, skidding off the dirt road under a huge elm. There wasn't a house in sight in front of him; nothing behind him but a slight turn in the road that left him exposed, alone—

He caught a flash of orange as he whipped his head around, throwing the thing that had touched his shoulder off and looking wildly into the back seat.

There was a pumpkin creature sitting there, calmly, regarding him with the empty holes of its eyes.

"Jesus—"

"I must talk with you," the thing said, as Grant fumbled for the door handle, pushed himself out of the car onto the ground, grabbing for his 9mm in its holster.

The pumpkin creature calmly opened the back door of the Taurus and stepped out.

Grant had the gun out, pointing it.

The pumpkin creature stepped calmly away from him a few feet, then settled on the ground, sitting Indian fashion.

It held a hand out toward him. "I only want to talk. And I don't have much time. You can call me John."

Grant thought he smelled the same fresh-cut pumpkin odor he'd smelled in town as the creature spoke.

"Please," the thing said.

"All right then, talk." Grant pushed himself into a crouching, then standing position, still aiming the 9mm.

"I understand you've met Samhain."

Grant said, tentatively, "Yes."

"That's why it's very important that I speak with you. This is going to be an extremely vital day, for all of us."

Grant said nothing, so the creature went on. "Corrie Phaeder is very important to your world, as well as mine. It's essential that nothing happens to him in this world today. Samhain will do everything he can to try to harm him, as well as a little girl named Regina Bright. If Samhain is able to harm or kill them today, I'm afraid both of our worlds will be—"

"What do you mean: both of our worlds? Where the hell are you from?"

The pumpkin stared at him. "The next world. The place humans go when they die."

"You're *dead*?"

"Of course. But I remember very little of my time on this world. I don't know who I was, for instance, when I lived on Earth."

224

Grant closed his eyes, then opened them. His mind was a mixture of numbness and crystal clarity.

After a moment, he said, "Isn't Samhain the Lord of the Dead?"

"Yes. In a way he's our master. But just as on Earth, when your master passes a line, does things that are detrimental to you, you fight back."

"Can't he destroy you?"

John gave a grim smile and tilted his head. "We're already dead. But the Dark One he works for is the opposite of you and I. You're life, and I am what comes after life. The Dark One wants only the annihilation of everything to do with life in the Universe. He is the Uncreator."

"What about the Creator?" Grant found himself saying. He suddenly felt as if he was back in bible school. "What about God?"

The pumpkin creature was silent for a long moment. Then he said, "I don't know."

"What the hell does that mean?"

"It means I don't know, just as you don't know. I doubt that Samhain knows, either. Being Death, he has been compelled to work for the Dark One. But even in him I've felt a certain reluctance, as though he feels that what he does is a perversion of his calling. In a way, he must know that if the Dark One succeeds, he too will cease to exist."

"The death of Death. He told me it would be a rest for him." Grant shook his head, still not believing the Alice in Wonderland conversation he was having with someone who claimed to be dead.

"Ever since I was in short pants I was taught that after death all the questions are answered . . ."

"There are just more questions, I'm afraid," the pumpkin creature said. "There is a place we inhabit that would seem very strange to you. It is a sort of way station. Sometimes some of us move on from it. But to where I have no idea, just as you don't." John leaned forward, almost eagerly. "Let me explain something to you, quickly. Here on Earth, all of the real supernatural occurrences, the ghost sightings, monsters, poltergeists—all of the things that Halloween has turned into a game— are the result of certain . . . minor overlaps between your world and mine. When something . . . supernatural happens here, it is because a momentary, and never permanent, crossing has taken place. We are the source of all your bogeymen, Detective Grant. Sometimes these crossings are benign, at other times they are less so. You must remember that everyone who dies on Earth crosses to this way station, the good and the bad."

John sat back. "Corrie Phaeder straddles both worlds, and so does the little girl I mentioned. We don't know why this happened, or who allowed it to happen, but for a long time we realized that Corrie, as a bridge between worlds, represented a way to battle the Dark One and prevent him from using my world as a stepping stone into yours, destroying all of us in the process. Tonight, Corrie Phaeder and Regina will cross from your world into mine alive, something that has never happened."

Grant, overwhelmed, said nothing.

"Already half of my world is gone," the pumpkin creature explained. He spread his hands, which were made of dried yellowed corn husks. "If Corrie and Regina cannot help, the Dark One will soon be here, where we sit in this pleasant place, and he will turn it, and all of this world, into . . . *nothing*."

Grant opened his mouth. "I—"

The creature held up a hand. "I need your help, Detective Grant. I need you to help protect Corrie and Regina until tonight at midnight. They are already partly into my world, and this offers them, as you will see, some amount of protection. Samhain will do everything he can, use any power he has, to try to stop them from completing the journey. He's already shown you what he is willing to do. He will not stop there."

"You visited me at my house, and when I chased you into the park . . ."

The pumpkin head nodded. "My calling card. To ready you for this meeting."

Grant said, "My wife Rose . . . she just died . . ."

John sighed. "I wish I could tell you something specific, Detective, but, as I said, when those of your world pass into mine, they lose all memory of their former standing. I can tell you that she is with us. But if we all fail tonight . . ."

"I don't believe this is happening."

"The things that will happen in the next few hours will seem like a nightmare. And they will be all too real. Remember that, Detective."

The light suddenly went out behind the pumpkin creature's eyes, nose, mouth. The voice became very grim. "I must go. Good-bye, Detective Grant."

Grant blinked, and the creature was gone.

Grant realized that he had been aiming his 9mm at the creature the entire time, his grip too tight, and that his hand was shaking.

On the ground where John had been, a sliver of dried corn husk rustled in the wind with fallen leaves, dervishing, then was still.

Chapter Twenty-nine

Halloween.

Orangefield, unaware of the greater drama, reveled in it, swam in it, put it on like a huge orange coat and pirouetted, showing it off. Bowls and plastic cauldrons were filled to the brim with fresh candy, waiting. Children, finally home from school, tried their costumes on for the fiftieth time, but this time kept them on, ready. Empty trick-or-treat bags, paper with handles, white pillow cases, fancy baskets painted black and orange, plastic pumpkins, were clutched in tiny hands, looking to be filled. Supermarkets ran low on eggs, shaving cream, toilet paper.

The day, hovering at an exact and perfect forty-eight degrees, moved into late-day. The sun arched over and began to fall. The blue sky deepened, turning leaves from bright golden and crimson to deeper roasted hues. The temperature, incrementally, began to drop toward chilly. A few lights blinked on, bright orange string lights across gutters, spotlights on front lawn tableaux: a papier-mâché spider caught in a huge rope web, a Frankenstein monster made of old clothes stuffed with newspaper. Carved pumpkins blinked on with candle light within, first one, then another, then a legion of porch dwellers. One house sported twenty lit pumpkins, all with different expressions, lined up along the front foundation. Another had twice that number lining the long curving driveway.

The town held its collective breath before launching into the day's reveries:

Then the first tentative toe (appropriately a girl in ballerina costume) set forth from the first house, followed by another and another until a flood of costumed miniature monsters and cartoon characters and celebrities past and present and the occasional hobo and spaceman, filled the sidewalks and spilled, excited and expectant, into the streets.

Halloween.

Orangefield jumped into it with both feet.

And, off in the far indistinct corners of the town, the darker places, the unvisited and inappropriate regions, the hollows, the gorges, the districts of rotting fallen trees and dampness, the hidden unwholesome areas, things stirred, and began, at the behest of the Lord of the Dead, to align and move . . .

Chapter Thirty

In the gloom of dusk, the front door to the Phaeder home was wide open.

Grant called out Corrie's name, but was met with silence. He took a step inside. There was no sound in the house—not a creak, the breath of wind through curtains, the snap of the same curtains in the breeze, a cough, a sniffle, a snore. It was as if the house was dead space.

He stepped all the way in and closed the door behind him.

Then Grant saw Corrie sitting in a chair in the living room.

At first he thought the boy was dead. He looked as if he had been placed in the chair the way a little girl places a rag doll. His arms rested on the arms, fingers curled down over the ends. His body was ramrod straight, his feet planted firmly on the floor. His head rested on the back of the chair as if he had fallen asleep. His face was bruised, his mouth open, eyes closed.

Something like a halo encircled his head.

Grant stepped into the living room, found a light switch and flipped it on. Nothing happened. He tried a nearby lamp, but the light failed to go on when he turned the switch.

It was cold in the room, and Grant closed the two open windows.

He approached the boy in the chair, reached out his hand—

The doorbell behind him went off—*DING-DONG!*—startling him to the point of jumping.

He retreated to the front door and opened it, his hand resting on his 9mm.

"Trick or treat!"

Two little pirates and a Snow White stood with open bags, staring up at him expectantly.

He rummaged in his pocket, brought out a handful of change, gave two of them quarters and the other one two dimes and a nickel.

They gave him a sour look and turned away.

Grant closed the door.

Corrie Phaeder still hadn't moved, and Grant was still not sure if he was alive or dead. He went back to the boy and reached out to touch him.

Something prevented him from doing so.

The vague halo of light around his head intensified. It was as if he was surrounded by some sort of force field. Grant thought about what the pumpkin man had said about Corrie being to some extent protected.

Corrie's eyes opened—they were black and empty, like two pools of inky black space—then closed.

Again the doorbell rang.

Grant went to it, opened it, pulling out his remaining change.

Three identically dressed goblins in head to toe costumes, green skin, ugly faces, pointed ears, clawed hands, large, hairy feet, stood there, bags in hand.

"All I have is pennies—" Grant began.

The three creatures rushed at him, knocking him down. He felt the weight of one of them, much heavier than a child.

Grant fought himself to his feet, but the creatures were past him, in the living room now, rushing at the figure of Corrie Phaeder in the chair.

Grant shouted at them but they ignored him. The one in front raised its claws, hissing, and ran straight at Corrie.

The goblin was thrown back, repelled by the force field.

The other two goblins were busy grabbing weapons—one snatched the lamp Grant had tried to turn on, yanking its cord out of the wall and marching toward Corrie with it. The third smashed a picture frame on a side table and tore out a long sliver of broken glass.

The one with the lamp beat at Corrie with no effect, the lamp base bouncing harmlessly off.

Grant had his revolver out.

The third charged screeching at Corrie with the glass sliver raised like a dagger. Grant shouted for it to stop but it ignored him.

Grant fired one shot, and the goblin disappeared in a flash of fire, leaving an odor like sulphur behind.

The other two renewed their attack on Corrie, and Grant fired a shot at each, making them disappear.

The room was filled with the stench of sulphur.

"Jesus," Grant breathed, lowering his gun.

He opened the windows, but quickly closed them again when he heard an ominous and growing buzzing sound.

The hair on the back of his neck stood up.

"Oh, shit."

Something rose from the other side of Sagett River—a huge dark amorphous cloud that flowed toward the house. Grant slammed the front door shut and ran from room to room, looking for opened windows, which he closed.

Upstairs he did the same, pushing aside a camera on a tripod in one room. As he closed the window something slammed against it like a fist. A solid wall of hornets hit the glass with a thousand taps and then flowed outward, looking for another way in.

Grant thought of the fireplace in the living

room, and ran back downstairs to see a cloud of insects flowing from the open hearth and surrounding Corrie like a cloud.

A second cloud broke away and flowed toward him, buzzing angrily.

He ran for the kitchen, looking madly for something to burn—the one thing he had learned from the bee keeper, Fred Willims, was that smoke would instantly turn hornets sluggish and harmless.

The kitchen sink was filled with dirty pans and dishes—Grant grabbed at a greasy-looking pot and turned a top burner on to high. As it began to heat and burn he added other greasy-looking items to it from the sink, then yanked open the refrigerator, pulling out the butter dish and emptying it into the mess.

The room began to fill with acrid smoke.

The fog of hornets reached out at him. A few individual insects, filled with rage, landed on his arms and then one found his face. It stung, then fell away.

The room was filling with thick smoke now. The cloud of hornets lost its energy. A smoke-detector somewhere went off. Grant grabbed at a magazine on the kitchen table and fanned the smoke out of the kitchen, into the rest of the house. In a few moments another smoke-detector went off, adding to the shrieking drone of the first.

The smoke reached into the living room, and the hornets began to settle away from Corrie's figure. He looked unharmed.

Grant looked through the windows.

The fog of insects was gone from the front of the house.

"We've got to leave," Grant said, not knowing if Corrie could hear him.

Grant went back into the kitchen, stepping over a carpet of dead and inert hornets. Choking, he reached out and turned off the burner, satisfied that the smoke would continue to pour from the mess in the pot for a while longer.

When he went back to the living room Corrie was standing, his eyes open. The insects had left him alone. A few confused rogues crawled aimlessly on the floor and walls.

"Corrie, can you hear me?"

Phaeder nodded.

"Then come with me."

Choking against the fumes, Grant led Corrie to the front door. He pulled it open quickly, stepping out and looking left and right. Clear.

"We're going to my car, Corrie. Get in as fast as you can."

Corrie gave him a single nod and followed Grant to the Taurus.

As Phaeder climbed into the back seat Grant heard a shriek from up Sagett Road.

"Now what," he mumbled, climbing into the driver's side and gunning the engine. He looked briefly back at the Phaeder house. Smoke was billowing from the open front door, but already lessening.

Past a thick stand of trees was a newer house.

The porch light was on, and two spots lit up the driveway. It, too, had been attacked by a cloud of hornets. Only this time they had been more successful. They covered the upper part of the house like a blanket, and were streaming into an open upper story window. A man lay unmoving on the front lawn, and a young woman, clutching what looked like a young girl, the upper part of her body covered by a blanket, stood over the man, screaming.

Grant watched the last of the hornets filter into the house, then almost immediately begin billowing out again.

Grant jumped out of his car and threw the back door open.

"Get in!" he ordered.

The woman looked up at him in shock.

"I can't touch my baby!" she moaned, and now Grant saw that the blanket kept sliding off the girl as if she were covered in grease.

"Is that Regina?" Grant asked.

She nodded weakly.

"Get into the car."

She moved toward it, obviously in shock.

Grant let the blanket fall to the ground and said to the girl, "Regina, Corrie is in my car. Will you go with him?"

She nodded; her eyes were as black and depthless as Corrie's.

"Go to the car."

She began to walk toward the Taurus.

Grant saw that the insects were beginning t
congregate into a thick cloud around the secon
story window.

He reached down and took the unconsciou
man under the arms and began to drag him towar
the automobile. The man's face was swollen, bu
he looked like he was breathing.

The woman was sitting in the front seat, starin
straight ahead, trembling. Her daughter sat besid
Corrie in the back seat, leaving just enough roor
for Grant to manhandle the unconscious form in
heap next to them.

The cloud, buzzing madly, started flowing tc
ward them.

Grant slammed the door shut, ran around to th
driver side and got in.

He threw the car into drive and made a shar
turn, kicking stones, and rammed down Sage
Road toward the main road. He was already on th
radio, telling the dispatcher to notify the hospit:
emergency room that two patients, one in need c
immediate attention for anaphylactic shock, wer
on the way.

At the end of Sagett Road Grant saw a dar
cloud waiting for them.

He slowed, and the car was suddenly sur
rounded by hornets.

They rose up from both sides of the road an
tore at the car, beating against the windows. Grar
gunned the engine, trying to ram through the fo;
but it kept pace and now he couldn't see. Horne

were crawling in through the vent system. Grant braked the car, twisting all the vent valves shut. The few that made it in were already stinging him. He fumbled in his pocket for a cigarette, jammed it into his mouth and lit it.

The hornets in the car went dormant as the smoke hit them.

Grant grabbed the radio and called in: "This is Bill Grant! I need immediate assistance on Sagett Road—repeat—"

"Is that you, Bill?" came Chip Prohman's laconic voice. "Did you know there's an a.p.b. out on you?"

"What?"

"Pell Johnson was in a little while ago and talked to the Captain, and they want your hide. Can't say I blame them, and I got you to thank for doing dispatch duty for three weeks—"

Grant tried to keep his voice reasonable. "Chip, I'm in big trouble—"

"I'll say you are. See you when they get you— you said you're on Sagett Road?"

"Never mind, you asshole."

Grant turned off the radio, jammed it into its cradle, and gunned the engine.

He threw on the windshield wipers, which gave him just enough vision to keep going.

The end of Sagett Road was in sight.

Miraculously, as he reached it, the hornets left the car in a cloud. He saw them disperse, looking suddenly lost, in his rearview mirror.

* * *

He did sixty, passing cars and leaning on his horn, all the way to the hospital.

The emergency room entrance was empty when he got there. He braked, tore open both doors on the passenger side, helped the woman out and then pulled the unconscious man out as gently as he could.

An orderly appeared, and Grant barked at him, "I'm a police officer. Get these two patients taken care of immediately. You should have been called by the police."

"Are you Detective Grant?" the orderly asked carefully.

"Yes. Why?"

"We had a call, but it was to ask you to come with us—"

Grant pulled his gun and pointed it at the orderly. "Take care of these two people. *Now*."

Grant saw two Orangefield police cruisers just edging onto the main road a good two blocks away.

"*Shit.*"

Grant holstered his gun, slammed both passenger side doors and ran around to his own side.

In a moment he had the car in gear and out on the main road.

To his relief, he saw the two cruisers pull into the hospital.

He hit the accelerator.

* * *

Five minutes later, on a road out of town, his cell phone went off.

He pulled it out, pushed the TALK button.

"Hello?" he said curtly, expecting someone from the police station.

"Detective Grant?" a languid, soft voice said. "This is Kathy Marks."

For a moment he went blank. Then he said: "Kathy, are you all right?"

There was silence which stretched to the point where Grant thought he had lost the connection. Then her voice came back: "I'm tired, Detective Grant. I just want to finally sleep."

"Kathy—"

She went on as if she hadn't heard him. "He's come back to me. He's promised to give me everything I want. He's promised to let me see my mother and father. That's all I ever really wanted. That and Corrie."

"Kathy, don't do anything until I get there. Promise me—"

She wasn't listening. She sounded infinitely tired. "Good-bye, Detective. He wants me to say good-bye. I'm so tired. And tell Corrie I loved him more than he ever knew."

The line went dead.

"Damn!"

Grant dropped the cell phone back into his pocket and hit the wheel in frustration with the flat of his hand. He dug furiously into his pocket and retrieved his notebook, flipping through it with one hand while trying to pay attention to the road ahead of him. In a moment he had located Kathy Marks's address.

He made a screeching U-turn, tore back the way he'd come for a half-mile, then took a side street named Parsons Road which neatly avoided the middle of town. In five minutes he was into the residential area of Orangefield, and in another minute was on her street.

Tires squealing, he hard-braked in front of her house and leaped out of the car, slamming the door behind him.

Out of breath, he came up short in the small back yard.

She was hanging from the single magnificent oak, from a sturdy branch, a spray of newly fallen leaves below her feet, which were suspended a yard off the ground. Her cell phone was nearby.

A step stool had been kicked over. Her face held the horrid, startled look of the asphyxiated, the dull blank look of surprise when taken-for-granted oxygen is removed.

Her hands had been tied behind her back, which puzzled Grant.

There came a sound from the far side of the house that drew Grant's attention, but then there was a louder one out front. Grant sprinted back around the house to see the car being assaulted by a gang of teenagers dressed in strips of clothing, their faces smeared with chalk-white makeup. They looked drugged.

One had the rear door of the Taurus open and was trying unsuccessfully to pull Regina out of the car.

Grant drew his gun and advanced on them, shouting, "Get away from the car."

From down the block was a larger group of teens, similarly dressed, some of them with base-ball bats.

The one pulling at the little girl whirled on him and hissed; the other two moved back at the sight of Grant's weapon but the third dropped Regina and sprang at Grant like a cat.

Grant hit him with the flat of the gun on the side of the face and he went down.

The other two continued to back toward the ad-vancing mob, melding into it. There was a growing angry sound coming from it, a low menacing hum like a generator revving up.

Grant moved to the car and slammed the rear door. He advanced on the front driver's side, bran-dishing his weapon.

Something sailed through the air at him from the middle of the crowd—a baseball bat, which hit the windshield and slid off. Grant climbed into the car and closed and locked the door.

Another stick flew at the car, hitting the passen-ger side windshield and making a crack. Now the crowd was rushing at them.

Grant turned the ignition, geared the car into drive and moved forward.

With an audible sigh the crowd tried to part, but Grant heard the solid smack of bodies not able to get completely out of the way. A hail of blows rained on the Taurus, and the rear driver's side window was smashed, then the rear windshield. One of the teens climbed onto the trunk and tried to get purchase on the broken window. Grant gunned the car and the boy slid away, howling.

Grant hit the accelerator and left the mob behind.

The barn was open, but Riley Gates's house had been shut up tight. Grant knew that Riley had relatives somewhere in Minnesota, a sister who had moved to Canada, but none of them had showed up for the funeral or come yet to claim Riley's possessions.

Grant hid the Taurus in the barn, going so far as to cover it with hay. It was a bad job, but would have to do.

He was able to get inside the house by breaking one small glass pane and opening a window. He herded his two passengers inside. Neither of them had uttered a word or made a gesture since he had got them into the car. When he told them what he wanted them to do, they nodded slightly and followed his directions.

He placed them in Riley's living room, which was spare but had a fireplace.

Grant patched the window pane he had broken. It was chilly in the house, and Grant soon discovered that the burner had been shut down and the water turned off.

He soon had both up and running, which was a good thing because he really didn't want to build a telltale fire.

The moon, like a huge silver coin, was climbing in the east.

Grant doubted that Riley would have any trick-or-treaters out here. Just to make sure, he stepped over the rutted long drive leading to the main road and replaced the gate with the CLOSED sign he had opened to get in. He studied the setup from the road—there was nothing to indicate that he was squatting here.

Thanks, podna, he thought.

He thought he caught movement out of the corner of his eye from Riley's pumpkin patch.

He stopped, studying the rutted, nearly empty field by moonlight. The only pumpkins left were rejects, deformed or rotted.

Grant waited a full minute, scanning the entire field, but saw nothing.

Must have been a crow.

He went back to the house, checking his gun as he did so. There had been an extra cartridge in the car, which he now had in his pocket, and a second which he always kept. Along with the cartridge in the 9mm, that made three.

In the house, he went to Riley's gun cabinet,

searched diligently for the key then ended up
hacking off the lock and hasp with a small hatchet
he found in the kitchen. Inside there was a shotgun, a .22 rifle and the Chinese version of the AK-
47, the latter without ammunition. But there were
plenty of shotgun shells, and enough .22 ammo to
start—or end—a small war.

Grant inspected and loaded everything, laying
the shotgun and rifle out on a side table.

The moon was hovering over the pick-your-own
pumpkin field now.

Something was outlined against it.

Something moving, flexing.

As Grant watched, a new figure rose up into
sight.

Could they have been lying down flat in the
field, waiting for him to pass? He definitely saw ar-
ticulated arms and legs.

The cops from the hospital?

But if so, where were their cruisers? There had
been no vehicles out on the road when he was
there.

Another figure rose, then another.

Grant's mouth opened in disbelief.

Three more rose straight up, and now as a group
they began to move toward the house, the moon
behind them.

Grant grabbed the .22, which had a telescopic
sight, and looked through it at one of the figures.

It had the head of an upside-down deformed

pumpkin, and a body similar in shape to the creature he had met.

But this one was made all of vines, twisted and gnarled into the shape of human limbs.

The pumpkin head had a cut-out face which flared into burning life—a down-turned, grim mouth and bright, too large eyes.

Grant lowered the rifle. More pumpkin men were rising, their misshaped heads flaring into life as they rose up out of the pumpkin field.

He turned the rifle scope on a particularly large deformed pumpkin, and watched it twist up off the ground into man-shape, dead vines twirling and shaping underneath it.

The first wave of the pumpkin army had reached the edge of the field, and moved toward the house.

One of them stooped to pick up something, a rock. Another now bore a long stick.

Others, Grant saw, were heading for the barn.

Grant slid up the window, and aimed through the crosshair sight at the nearest, who glared at him with pure hate.

He pulled the trigger and the head exploded in a shower of orange pieces.

The vines underneath the head collapsed and lay still on the ground.

Grant pulled off two more shots, but the pumpkin men were already learning. One crouched out of his line of sight behind Riley's pay booth, and a second was running.

He was able to hit another and then another, but by now the pumpkins were scattering, splitting into groups and beginning to surround the house.

"Don't suppose you could help, Corrie?" Grant said, checking the young man and the girl, who sat quietly, their eyes open and deep, vacant black.

The field of view in front of Grant was empty, and then he heard a shatter of glass at the rear of the house.

He ran that way, grabbing the shotgun from the table, and went into Riley's bedroom just as a second rock came through another window pane. One of the monsters was reaching in to unlock the latch. Grant fired two barrels at it, shattering the window and the pumpkin man at the same time. Grant reloaded as another figure took the first's place. Grant stepped farther into the room and shot it as it tried to snake a vine-like foot through the ragged opening.

Down the short hall, at the rear of the house, another window broke.

This is not working.

Another shatter of glass, this time from the front of the house.

Grant ran back to the living room in time to see two shattered windows, and pumpkin men climbing through the ragged openings.

"Corrie! Regina! Come with me!"

The boy and young girl rose from their chairs and turned toward him.

Grant dropped the first pumpkin man who

climbed all the way into the window; from down the hall behind him he heard another and turned in time to hit him with his second shotgun shell. Another appeared behind it from the bedroom and Grant hit it twice with his 9mm, finally cutting its head into chunks of blasted pumpkin.

He thought of the cellar—then thought better of it—he remembered that there were casement windows down there and decided on the attic, where Riley's Lionel trains were. There were no windows up there.

The pull-down stairs were in the hallway. Glancing behind to see that Corrie and the girl were making their way toward him, he ran farther down the hall, locating the pull cord just past Riley's spare bedroom. He transferred his gun from his right hand to left and yanked it down. The panel stuck, and Grant yanked harder, breaking off the wooden handle from the rope. He jumped and wrapped his wrist around the rope higher up, pulling downward with all his weight.

It edged downward—

He heard a sound behind him. He turned to see a pumpkin creature reaching out for him, another behind him between himself and the two young people, who stood mutely at the end of the hall.

Grant shouted and uncoiled his hand from the rope, switching his 9mm from his left hand back to his right and firing point blank into the pumpkin's head. It exploded in a shower of pieces. The second pumpkin was moving toward the two young people, and Grant leaped at it, tackling it. Immediately the vines that formed its body began to coil around him like live snakes, collapsing its body onto him. He felt the gun being pressured from his hand, and looked directly into the madly grinning face on the pumpkin.

With all his might, he dropped down on the monster's head, driving it into the floor.

With a sickening squashing sound, the head imploded and he was suddenly free as the vines went limp, losing all life.

Another pumpkin had climbed through Riley's window, and there were two behind Corrie and the girl.

Grant shot the first, then sprinted to the young man and girl and pulled them farther up the hallway. He shot over them at the two closest figures, noting that a mob of pumpkin men was now in the living room moving resolutely toward them. He fired a volley of shots into them. Three went down. Then his gun clicked on empty.

He pulled the empty cartridge out, reached into his pocket for another and jammed it into place. Again he fired a volley. More pumpkin men were climbing through the windows, and now the door was open, letting even more in. The front of the house was a sea of pumpkin heads.

"Corrie, Regina, come on!"

He turned and ran to the overhead stair panel, dropping another pumpkin man in Riley's bedroom and then leaping to put his fingers under the wide crack of an opening his efforts had gained him. The panel moved down another inch before his fingers slipped.

Again he jumped, wrapping his wrist around the cord again, and this time the entire panel came most of the way down with a creaking groan, almost hitting him. He pulled it the rest of the way and grabbed at the folded ladder, forcing it down.

"Corrie!"

The boy was behind him, and Grant herded him onto the ladder and he began to climb.

Regina had disappeared.

Grant fired wildly into Riley's bedroom as he passed, then ran to the end of the hallway.

Two pumpkin men were trying to carry Regina toward the front of the house. Their vines kept slipping away from her, but they were forming a basket of more and more vines around her, enclosing her completely.

Grant hit the first and as his head exploded half the basket dissolved. Another pumpkin man and then another immediately took its place.

Grant kept firing until the girl was free. She stood in a mass of inert vines.

"Regina, walk toward me—quickly!"

The girl did as he was told. Grant covered her with fire until she finally reached him.

"Now go to the ladder and climb!" Grant ordered.

She walked past him and went to the ladder.

Again Grant was out of ammo. He reached into his pocket for his third and final clip.

He hammered it home, turning in time to prevent a pumpkin man just leaving Riley's bedroom from accosting Regina.

Grant destroyed him, and then was climbing up the ladder after the girl.

There was a light switch mounted on a bare rafter and Grant flipped it on. The attic flared into light.

Grant pulled the panel up after him, sealing them off from the lower part of the house.

Almost immediately there came a dull pounding on the panel.

To his relief, as Grant had thought, there were no dormers up here, no other entrances. The attic was semi-finished, bare rafters at one end and a beautiful train room at the other. Riley's train board ran around one entire end of the attic in a U shape. There were miniature towns, one with a painted lake dressed in spring colors on one side and the other dusted with white artificial snow. Two trains, a diesel freight and a line of New York Central passenger cars, pulled by a beautiful Hudson steamer, sat on separate tracks waiting to be run, one at each end of the layout. Riley's other trains were neatly boxed and stacked next to the board.

The poundings from below increased. Grant watched the panel move downward an inch.

He circled around Corrie and Regina, who had

ettled onto the floor next to one another. Their
yes, filled with black, looked big as saucers.

The panel creaked again, moved down another
nch.

Grant rummaged under the train board and lo-
ated a tool box. There was a hammer, but no
ails.

"Shit."

More pounding on the panel, a creaking
ound—

Grant went to the other end of the attic and
icked out a cross stud in the bare rafters. He furi-
usly beat on it with the hammer, getting it to
oosen.

There were two nails in each end, and Grant
oon had a ready-to-use piece of lumber in his
ands.

He went back to the panel and yanked it up into
osition, cutting off a green vine which had
naked up through the opening. He hammered the
tud into position crosswise over the panel, ham-
nering one end into the door itself and the other
nto the plywood floor of the attic.

He retreated to the bare end of the attic again,
nd repeated the operation twice. For good mea-
ure, he located a longer stud and wedged it side-
vays through an opening in the folded ladder, then
ammered the stud into the floor, effectively brac-
ng the panel in place.

The poundings on the panel continued—but
ow it didn't move.

Grant sat down, sweating and gasping.

"Well, gang," he said, "we're safe—for now."

Corrie Phaeder and Regina Bright stare straight ahead.

Grant looked at his watch.

It was ten to nine.

Chapter Thirty-one

"You've been a great disappointment to me so far."

Pell Simpson cowered in the farthest corner of his dark basement. He had stripped himself naked; his face was blotched with crying; there was a bruise on his forehead where he had driven his head into the cold cinder block wall behind him.

"Does this fetal position help you?" the voice said. It was both amused and perplexed. "I must say, as long as I've studied your kind, I can never quite figure out all of your symbols and practices. Do you feel cleaner now, or dirtier?"

"Dirty. I feel dirty."

"And that's good?"

"I've done a bad thing." He began to tremble and balled his hands over his eyes, crying and rocking back and forth.

"You've done a lot of bad things, Pell. You've been doing bad things since you were ten years old. Don't you remember what you used to do to cats when you were ten, Pell?"

Simpson nodded, continuing to rock back and forth on his haunches. "I was bad then, too."

"Yes, that was the first time we met. But you got over it, didn't you? Or, rather, you learned how to hide it, just as I showed you to. Didn't I show you how to manage your need to control things?"

Pell sniffled, pulling his hands away from his eyes.

"Didn't I show you how to get away with things? To wear masks? To be what you needed to be?"

Pell was drying his eyes, now. "Yes, you did."

"I've always been good to you, haven't I, Pell?"

"I didn't know you were Samhain."

In front of him, in the gloom of the cellar, outlined in a faint rectangle of light from the single window on the far wall, the flapping cloak and ghostly pale gray face appeared.

"Who did you think I was, Pell?"

"I thought you were *me*."

Samhain laughed, a not unkind sound. "Oh, don't brag, so, Pell. You never thought that at all. You're not that stupid. You weren't sure exactly what I was, inside or out of your head—but then you didn't much care, did you?"

Pell took a shuddering breath and answered, "No."

"That's more like it. The truth. The only thing that mattered was that you got what you needed.

That you found animals that no one would miss, and later itinerants that no one would miss, and after that young girls out on the main highway, runaways who would get into a police car who no one would miss. Wasn't it me who told you to join the police force in the first place, Pell?"

"Yes."

"And was I right? Do you know how many policemen are sadists, and . . . others with your . . . special needs? You'd be surprised if I told you, I think. There was another on your own force, for instance . . ."

Pell was consumed by curiosity now. "Really?"

"Yes. He's no longer there—"

"Atkins," Pell said immediately. "He was dismissed last year. We all knew there was something off with him."

The cloak hung still, and the face hovered, a gray ghost in the cellar. "Very good, Pell. You're broadening your perspective. And you'd be surprised how many other men and women in Orangefield I've . . . helped over the years."

Pell continued to stare at Samhain with interest. "Who?"

Samhain chuckled. "You already know about Marvin Soames. The others I can't tell you about. Trade secrets, you know. Detective Grant is certainly not one of them."

"No."

"And speaking of Detective Grant . . ."

Pell began to get nervous again. He was no longer crying, but he started to rock back and forth on the balls of his feet. "I don't know . . ."

"Didn't I always tell you I might need you for something like this? In return for all the good things I've done for you?"

"I took care of Soames in his cell for you, I took care of the librarian . . ."

"You were right there with me for Kathy, making sure it went as planned, that's true. You have to admit that after the pills you gave her she was ready for anything I told her. All you did was help her with the rope.

"But I wanted you to take care of Grant and the boy and girl then, and instead you hid on the side of the house and watched as they came and went."

"I like Bill Grant! He was my friend . . ."

"Aren't *I* your friend, Pell? Wasn't *I* your friend when no one else was? When your mother . . ."

Pell put his hands to his ears and screamed. *"Don't ever talk about my mother!"*

"Why not, Pell? You had no qualms about Corrie Phaeder's mother, when the time came and I asked you to—"

"That was different! SHE WASN'T MY MOTHER!"

"That's true. But have you forgotten, Pell? Forgotten what happened with your mother?"

"No! No!" Pell screamed, smashing his hands into his ears.

"Time you remembered, Pell . . ."

Twelve years old, and his mother found him with the Jurgens girl.

Not like it was the first time, but this time she caught him red-handed, as she would say. Out behind the shed, poking the four-year-old girl with a sharp stick after he had hit her on the head with a rock and knocked her out. Then he had wrapped plastic wrap around the girl's face, and waited.

She caught him when she came out looking for a rake from the shed, and the girl was still alive.

His mother's face turned the brightest red he had ever seen, and she hit him so hard he literally left his feet and landed in a heap.

"What in God's name are you doing!" she screamed, and tore into the girl, kneeling on the ground, ripping the plastic wrap from her head and shaking her. Then she saw the bloodied lump on the girl's head and lay her down and hit him again with her fist as he started to get up.

"You little sick bastard! I can't believe you came out of me! What have you done!"

The girl coughed then, and began to choke and then she vomited. His mother went to her again, cradled her head, and put her fingers into the girl's mouth to clear it out. Then she turned the girl sideways and smacked her on the back.

The girl continued to cough, and then gasped and opened her eyes. For a moment she looked at nothing but then she turned her head and looked up at his mother and began to cry.

His mother began to rock her, soothing, "Oh, darling, darling it's all right now," and it was then that Pell picked up another rock and hit his mother on the back of the head, bringing it down with both hands as hard as he could.

She collapsed in a heap with a groan on top the girl and then Pell hit the girl with the rock and then his mother again, alternating until they were both quiet.

He wrapped both their heads with plastic wrap and waited, counting to five hundred.

Then he took the plastic wrap off and put a shard of a mirror he kept under their noses and when it didn't cloud he was sure. It had always worked on the animals.

He balled up the plastic wrap and put it in his pocket, then went into the house.

Sure enough, his stepfather was asleep in his rocker in front of the television. Pell went to the hall closet and got his winter gloves out and put them on, then he went to their bedroom and took his stepfather's pistol out of the second dresser drawer and brought it back and held it to the right side of his stepfather's head and pulled the trigger.

His stepfather's snoring stopped immediately, and his head fell over that way. Pell put the gun in his right hand and let it fall into his lap. Then he took out the two wads of plastic wrap and pressed them into his stepfather's left hand.

He took off his gloves, put them back in the hall closet, and ran all the way to the police station in town, screaming.

* * *

"Of course you killed her, Pell. You killed her and I was there and told you what to do. If I hadn't, you wouldn't be here now. They would have put you away, and you never would have been able to control anything again."

Pell said nothing, his eyes tightly closed, his hands still over his ears. Then his rocking lessened, and he was still.

"Do you want to be found out now, Pell? Especially with all the bodies you have buried in this cellar?"

"No."

"They can still put you away forever. They might even do worse to you, considering all the things you've done since then."

Slowly, Pell nodded.

"Is Bill Grant worth that, Pell? Is anybody worth your freedom, and your control?"

In a small, quiet voice, he answered, "Nobody's worth that."

"That's what I thought. Now clean yourself up, and get dressed. I could have you tell your Captain Farrow where Detective Grant is and have him handle it, but I don't think that would work. There are too many things that could go wrong. I want you to handle it yourself, in your own way. If you do, you can even have the young girl, if you want.

"Put on your cleanest suit, and strap on your shoulder holster. Here's what I want you to do . . ."

Chapter Thirty-two

The house was quiet.

Grant cursed the fact that there were no dormer windows in the attic—a fact which he had been thankful for a few hours before. The noises at the pull-down stairs had continued unabated—Grant had even heard banging on other parts of the ceiling below, which meant that the pumpkin creatures were trying to find another way up to the attic.

But then, suddenly, an hour ago, they had gone silent, and had stayed that way.

Grant almost began to relax.

It was now well past eleven o'clock. The moon would be up high. In town, the Halloween festivities would be at their height, before the curfew at twelve o'clock went into effect and the streets emptied. This was usually the time when the egg-throwing teens came out, and toilet paper was wrapped around trees in Rainer Park. His own mailbox was probably filled with shaving cream by now. He had no doubt there were eggs dripping down his windows, because he was not home giving out candy as was demanded.

If that was my only problem, he thought, and almost laughed.

Corrie Phaeder and the girl hadn't moved. They sat side by side on the floor, their eyes huge black holes into another world. They had begun to exude a weird sound, a hum almost, and their skin looked hot to the touch. If Grant hadn't lived through everything he had the last few hours, and hadn't seen the things he'd seen with his own eyes, he would have rushed them to the hospital.

Instead he sat locked in an attic (and a stuffy one at that) guarding them from an army of evil pumpkin men and the Lord of Death because someone who claimed to be dead made out of corn stalks with a smiling pumpkin for a head had told him to.

He remembered what John had told him, that what happened would seem like a nightmare . . .

He shook his head.

Extremely weird shit.

His cell phone rang.

The sound in the attic, faint as it was, was startling. There hadn't been a sound of any kind but Grant's own breathing and the weird low hum from the young man and kid for so long—

He pulled the phone out of his pocket and jabbed a finger at TALK.

"Bill? That you?"

Almost simultaneously, he heard a sound below him, a rattle and bang toward the front of the house that was echoed on the phone.

It was Pell Simpson.

"Are you here, Farmer?"

"I'm standing right inside the front door. What in hell happened here?"

Grant sighed. "You wouldn't believe me if I told you."

"Well try me—the damn floor is covered with vines and pieces of pumpkin—"

"Did you see anything alive when you came in? Anything outside. . . ?"

"You mean like a dog—"

"Anything at all, Farmer."

"No. Quiet as a church on Tuesday down here. And where the hell *are* you?"

"I'm—"

Something in Pell Simpson's voice, something in the back of Grant's head that went off with a faint warning *buzz*, made him hesitate.

"How did you know I was here, Farmer?" Grant asked.

Momentary silence. Then: "Cruiser saw your car turn in here hours ago and called it in."

"You sure about that?"

"Saw the log myself. Captain Farrow wants to talk to you *bad*, podna."

The warning buzz was still sounding. Something was different about Farmer's voice, his manner—there was an edge, a sharp wariness in it that Grant had never heard before.

"I'm sure he does. You here to arrest me— *podna*?"

There was still sound from downstairs: footsteps, occasional bangings and thumps.

Farmer laughed on the other end of the phone. "Nothing so drastic, Bill. Just need to figure this all out, is all."

"Figure what out?"

"There's a kidnaping charge out on you, for some little girl named Regina Bright. Seems you left her parents standing outside the emergency room at Orangefield General and took their daughter."

The shuffling sounds were getting closer and quieter. Grant could imagine Farmer in the hall now, moving closer—

Grant waited a moment. "What would you say if I told you I had to do it?"

Farmer hesitated. "I'd say you needed a pretty damn special reason and we should talk about it face to face."

The sounds stopped somewhere just below him.

Pell said, "Jesus, look at this shit! There's a pile of twisted dead vines and pumpkin halves piled halfway to the ceiling—"

Some deeper gut instinct in Grant allied with a familiar sound from below made him push himself away from the pull-down ladder as a blast of shotgun pellets came up through the floor. The far side of the wooden ladder splintered into pieces. Grant covered his face and kept crabbing backwards as another blast took off another chunk of ladder. Wood flew by his head and he was stabbed in the arm by a long sliver which he immediately yanked out.

He stopped and glanced at Corrie Phaeder and Regina, who sat staring straight ahead, unfazed . . .

Another blast rocked the floor in front of him, followed by a settling silence.

"Bill? Do I have your attention?"

Amazed, Grant realized that he still clutched the cell phone to his ear.

He said nothing.

"Doubt I hit you, but that wasn't the intention, old buddy. I'm supposed to take the boy and girl in with me is all."

"Take them in to who?"

"To *me*."

Grant turned with a gasp to see the floating, softly flapping cloak of Samhain, not three feet away from him. Samhain was staring in a kind of wonder at Corrie and Regina, his mouth open, showing a similar empty blackness to the one in their eyes.

Grant glanced at his watch: it was 11:50.

"This is remarkable," Samhain said, before turning his attention almost reluctantly back to Grant. "Truly remarkable." There was almost pride in his voice. "To think those in my world

267

could get this far . . ." The mouth closed like a trap. "But humans are, in the main, inefficient creatures." In a louder voice he called: "The same direction, Pell, but three feet on."

Grant reacted immediately, scrambling back as the sound of a shotgun cocking came from below followed immediately by a blast just in front of him. He kept moving as Samhain called out directions. Grant moved to the left and right as he scrambled back toward the train table, yelling at Corrie and Regina to do likewise. They nodded vaguely and rose to follow him.

Grant pointed his own shotgun at Samhain and watched the blast pass harmlessly through him.

"Can't kill Death, my friend," Samhain said calmly, before calling out more directions below. Grant could hear Pell stomping around from room to room below him; he quickly visualized the plan of the first floor and imagined Farmer must now be in the kitchen.

A blast tore up, right through the train table, destroying track and scattering the freight train. Grant angled his own shotgun down into the hole and fired it.

There was a titter of laughter from below.

"Missed me, podna!"

"Move to the extreme far wall!" Grant ordered, and the children obeyed. Samhain turned to watch their tandem progress.

"Inefficient, but sometimes ingenious creatures. You know that area downstairs is cluttered with support beams and walls for the back of the house behind the patio. Difficult for our moronic friend to do his business."

He turned his cold empty eyes on Grant. "And you know by now that I can't directly harm you. I've noticed that the boy and girl are already partly in my world, which has clothed them in a shield of sorts. But they can still be harmed by something, shall we say, drastic."

Another blast rocked through the train table, blowing up one end where the artificial lake had been painted. Tiny painted water skiers and plastic boats flew into the air.

"Pell," Samhain called in a loud voice, "turn on all the burners on the kitchen stove and then run out to the barn. Riley Gates kept dynamite out there for getting rid of tree stumps. Bring all of it into the kitchen. And *hurry*, Pell."

There came a shout of assent from below.

Grant looked again at his watch: 11:54.

"Six more minutes," Samhain assured him. "And then they will pass from here to my own world. And if that happens, they will deal with something far worse than me, Mr. Grant."

"But then you might lose."

Grant, sure that Pell had left, went quickly to the access panel and tried to remove the studs he had nailed across it to keep it in place. He couldn't locate the hammer. Samhain was floating nearby, chuckling, watching him.

"Not enough time. But for me, I think, there is."

Grant spied the hammer, next to one of the shotgun holes, under a pile of splinters.

He reached out for it and a green vine snaked up from below, snatching it down and away.

Samhain chuckled again. "I still have a few tricks of my own, Mr. Grant."

The vine continued to rise, and a pumpkin head rose into view in the opening.

Grant turned his shotgun around and butted the head into pieces. It fell back into the hole, the green vine snaking down after it.

Grant's watch said 11:56.

He heard banging around down below.

"Got the dynamite!" Pell called up, almost happily.

"Put it in a pile on the kitchen table. And light it."

Desperately, Grant reloaded his shotgun. Breathing heavily, he ran to the boy and girl.

Samhain was gone, but Grant heard muffled voices downstairs, Samhain's orders and Pell's replies of "Okay."

Grant told the boy and girl to move aside, and they stepped together out of his way.

He aimed his shotgun at the floor behind where they had been standing, which was over the patio, and fired off both shots.

A six-inch ragged hole formed.

He quickly reloaded, firing again.

The hole widened, showing Riley's back porch, the white wicker chairs still arranged next to the table.

Grant reloaded, shot, reloaded, shot.

He butted the hole wider.

Again he reloaded, shot, again, then reached back into his pocket and discovered he had only one more shell.

He pushed it into the chamber, closed it, and widened the hole a little more. The girl could now it through.

Samhain appeared next to him, his mouth opening to say: "In another few moments—"

His voice flared into rage as he watched Grant order the girl into the opening. She dropped onto the wicker chair below.

"What are you doing!"

"Now walk into the field, away from the house!" Grant ordered her.

He began to hammer at the hole with the stock of the shotgun, widening it still further.

Corrie Phaeder followed the girl down.

Grant eased himself into the opening, snagging for a moment on a ragged edge of plywood. He could feel it ripping into his thigh.

He looked back at Samhain.

"I have a few tricks left, too," Grant said, and dropped down onto the chair.

He hobbled after the boy and girl, who were halfway to the edge of the pumpkin field. Coming toward them were more pumpkin men, their glowing eyes filled with rage.

Grant looked behind: he saw Samhain flowing through the attic opening after him, mouth open in a scream, and Pell Simpson trying to climb from the kitchen window as something ignited behind him and then flared into brilliance like the noonday sun.

The house trembled—then there was a huge explosion which threw Grant to the ground.

He covered his head until the rumblings stopped.

He looked up to see Samhain in front of him hovering over Corrie Phaeder and Regina Bright the pumpkin men surrounding them—

Grant looked at his watch—

It was midnight—

"Noooooooooooooooo!" Samhain screeched, as the vines collapsed under the pumpkin men. Their heads fell to the ground, cracking open.

Grant stared at the spot where the boy and girl had been.

It was empty.

Samhain turned to look at him for the briefest moment. His eyes were wide with what looked like fear and his mouth was open in an empty circle of despair.

"It—" he said.

Then he was gone, melted away into the suddenly quiet Halloween night. Behind Grant, the destroyed house was still.

Grant kept staring at the empty spot.

"My God," he said, putting his head down to the ground and closing his eyes. "What the hell just happened?"

272

Chapter Thirty-three

Where—

"Mommeeee?"

Where—

The sky opened up in front of him. It was mustard yellow, banked with odd, low, sickly gray clouds.

He stood on a high bluff. A dry, stale wind, antiseptic-smelling, blew past him. It desposited a think layer of gritty silt at his feet. The air tasted dry as toast, weak in oxygen.

"Mommeeee?"

He looked down to see the girl huddled on the ground, shivering, her eyes closed tightly.

"It's me, Reggie. Corrie. Open your eyes."

She did so, blinking. Her eyes were still pitch-black, filled with darkness. Her hair had turned bone white. Reggie noticed that the thin hairs on his arms and the back of his hands had done the same.

"Where are we, Corrie?"

"I have a pretty good idea."

Corrie patted her head, as she closed her eyes again and began to whimper.

It looked different than it had in the dreams, or whatever they had been. He imagined that when they had been examining it from the balloons it was a mixture of Earth and this world. Now it looked totally alien, like another planet, only once removed from reality. It was like looking at an exposed negative, everything stark and too bright.

He looked up. There was no sun, but the yellow sky held a singular bright illumination. He wondered if there was a version of night.

"I can't breathe right," Reggie complained. She had opened her eyes again, and now she stood up next to him. She took his hand and held it very tight. "When I try to breathe it sticks like in the back of my throat and I don't think it's getting to my lungs can you—"

"Shhhh," Corrie said, smiling inwardly at her resilience: already she was reverting to her run-on manner of speaking. "Be quiet, Sniffles. Just breathe normally, only pull the air in slowly and a little bit deeper."

"Okay I will but I don't know if it will work who is Sniffles?"

"You're Sniffles."

"But I don't sniffle I—"

274

"Shhh, and do what I say."

She was quiet, and Corrie heard her breathing, practicing what he had told her.

The bluff they stood on led down a gentle slope to something on Earth that would have resembled a river. But it was chalky-looking and he could detect no movement of water. To either side of it were stubby trees and, far in the distance, where the river wound to, a thicker grove of trees, yellow-green in color. The ground was desert-like, but pocked with different colors of tan, some light, some darker. Clusters of boulders and rocks protruded from the silt and, far to his right, where the land dipped down even lower, he saw the top of what looked like a structure, flat-topped and wide, with a single tall spire.

I guess we should head that way, he thought.

At the far horizon was a black thin smudgy line which ran halfway across his vision; it was upset here and there by rises of what looked like thunderheads.

Corrie studied them for a few moments, remembering the black, eaten-away sky in the dreams—

"Come on, Reggie. Time to go."

"All right, Corrie, I think I can breathe now boy your hair is white I guess mine is too—"

He smiled down at her.

"You look weird, Corrie—"

"So do you, Reggie. Come with me."

He clutched her hand and led her down the slope to the valley below.

They walked for what Reggie estimated to be an hour, stopping frequently due to lack of breath. When they got to the floor of the valley there was more perspective to the landscape: rock shapes took on three dimensions, and the "river" proved to be filled with something that looked, and tasted, like salt. The structure he had seen from above disappeared behind a canyon wall, but he had marked the direction and they continued that way.

It occurred to him that, except for his own voice and Reggie's, he had not heard a single sound since they got here. Even the wind was silent, though it did stir up dust devils and blow something that looked almost like tumbleweed across the landscape. The air was oppressively dry and Corrie was surprised to find that he was hungry.

"I want a drink of water, Corrie," Reggie complained, after what Corrie estimated to be another hour of trekking.

"I'm with you, kid," Corrie answered. "Got any ideas?"

She stared around. "The river had no water but maybe there's some underground like the oasis in the movies I remember—"

"That's enough, Reggie. Let's look for a cluster of bushes or trees and try there."

She nodded.

She proved to have better eyes than him, and in a few moments was pointing to a not-too-distant cluster of plants.

"There!"

"Good enough. Let's check it out."

When they reached the plants, which were far-ther away than they had looked, Corrie's hopes sank. There were five reedy, yellow-green pieces of vegetation, but they looked too scrawny to mark water. He yanked one out of the ground, and noted its wide, flat root system.

"Here!" Reggie called out, and when Corrie reached her, on the far side of the cluster, he found a shallow gray pool of what resembled water.

"Let me," he said, bending down to scoop up the liquid, which looked like quicksilver in his palm.

He brought it to his lips and tasted.

It was water, brackish but, to his surprise, al-most cold.

"It's okay, Reggie."

"Hurrah!" She knelt down and put both hands into it, making a cup and drinking.

"So we know there's water here," Corrie said out loud. "I wonder if there's food, too. Are you hun-gry, Reggie?"

"Yes!"

Corrie eyed the plant he had yanked out of the ground, breaking off a thin branch and tentatively biting it.

"Phoo." He spit it out. It tasted acidic and bitter.

"Try this end!" Reggie called. She already had picked up one of the shallow, thin roots, and nib-bled on it. "Tastes like celery!"

Corrie followed her example. It did, indeed,

277

taste something like celery, more like scallions, almost sweet.

They finished their meal, and Corrie stuffed some of the roots into his pocket.

"Feel okay, Reggie?"

She nodded, and Corrie noted no ill effects from the meal himself.

"Then let's keep walking."

They resumed their trek toward the structure.

On Earth, if they had started in the early morning, Corrie reckoned that it would now be late afternoon. Periodically, he had stopped to turn and mark the bluff from which they had started, and though it looked farther away each time, finally blending into the landscape behind them, they seemed to be making little progress forward. The wall of rock hiding the structure he had seen looked to be as far away as when they set out.

After another hour or so of walking, Corrie stopped and said, "You tired, Reggie?"

"Yes."

As she said so she yawned, and Corrie added, "Then let's stop here to sleep."

Without hesitation, she curled up on the ground next to him and in a few moments was asleep.

Amazing, Corrie thought. *She was probably worn out an hour ago, but waited until I said to stop. And then instantly asleep.*

Corrie monitored his own stamina, and found

that though he was weary, he knew he would not be able to sleep.

He sat down next to Reggie, pulled a stub of the onion root out of his pocket and chewed on it thoughtfully.

So this is where you go when you're dead.

The sky, the landscape, the brightness of the sky, nothing had changed a bit since he'd gotten here. Was this what eternity was like? Eternal . . . sameness? If there was, indeed, a place beyond this one, as John had hinted, was it the same as this? If this was just a way station, was the real afterlife anything better? He sure as hell hoped so. It hardly seemed worth dying to get here.

If this was the Kingdom that Samhain ruled, Corrie almost felt sorry for him.

Not much being Lord of the Dead, if this was what you lorded over.

And what about the dead? Where were they? Where was John, and all the weird-shaped beings he and Reggie had seen in their dreams?

Corrie found himself yawning. He had been more tired than he thought.

He looked down at Reggie, peacefully asleep, and wondered what he and she were. Were they dead? Alive? Something in-between? He had been hungry and thirsty enough. He doubted that when you were dead you had to eat, or drink, or . . .

He yawned again, and walked a discreet distance away from the sleeping girl to relieve himself.

So you can piss in the afterlife, he thought, and almost laughed.

He walked back to the girl and lay down on the silty desert floor.

He yawned yet again.

And then, like a light switch being thrown, he was asleep.

Chapter Thirty-four

"I don't know whether to arrest you, shake your hand or shoot you," Captain Farrow growled.

Grant stood on the other side of the captain's desk. He had refused to sit down. He was dog tired, and all he wanted to do was sleep, but instead he was here being grilled in an interview that might end with handcuffs on his wrists. He had noted the jackal's look on the face of Chip Prohman, who was back on duty as desk sergeant.

"I can keep telling you one thing, and that's what happened," Grant said.

To his surprise, Farrow didn't hit the roof. Instead, he got up, walked around his desk to the office door and closed it.

"Sit down, Bill. Please," he said, his voice low and serious.

Intrigued, Grant slowly lowered himself into the chair he had been standing in front of, while the captain settled back into his own. Farrow picked a pencil up and studied it.

"How well did you know Pell Simpson?" Farrow asked.

Grant shrugged. "Well as your know somebody you work with, I guess. He was a little reserved, but I've seen worse."

Like an actor, Farrow waited two beats before replying. "I have no doubt that he tried to kill you, just like you said. We visited his house yesterday, after the . . . incident out at Riley Gates's farm, and found some interesting evidence of what he'd been up to for quite a long time."

Grant waited.

Farrow turned in his chair and put the pencil down. "Now I know why they called him Farmer," the captain said. "He had bodies planted all over his basement, all over his property."

Grant opened his mouth to speak but Farrow held a hand up. "Nobody knows this but you and me, and the two guys I sent out there yesterday . . . and the mayor. Do you know what it would do to the department and this town if it got to the papers that we had a serial murderer on the force? If it got to television? It would destroy Orangefield, and all of us with it."

Now Farrow waited for Grant to speak, but he said nothing.

"This is the deal," the captain said, slowly and evenly. His eyes never left Grant's. "You keep quiet about this, and nothing happens to you. Nothing.

There are about eighteen things you did that I don't understand, and now I don't want to understand them. Regina Bright's parents we can handle. I promised to call in the FBI to find their daughter. I will—eventually. They're acting half nuts anyway, with all their paranormal claims, and we've got them isolated in Killborne at the moment. As far as I'm concerned, Corrie Phaeder abducted her, and that's the way we're going to play it. The fact that you helped Phaeder at one point will have to be explained, but, at the mayor's request, I'm working on it.

"On the other hand," Farrow went on, and now the familiar nasty bulldog spark was in his eyes as he put his folded hands on his desk and leaned forward, "if you throw a wrench into anything Mayor Gergen or I am doing, if you go to the press, if you even think bad thoughts for the next chunk of forever, you'll be in Killborne yourself"—here Farrow almost faltered, and Grant knew he was remembering Grant's wife Rose, and trying to deal with it, which he did by just plowing ahead—"and then hoeing pumpkins for a living because you'll never be a cop here or anywhere else again." He leaned back in his chair and turned his attention back to his pencil. "Clear?"

"Clear as glass," Grant said.

Captain Farrow looked at him with surprise. "You're okay with this?"

Grant forced a grim smile onto his face. "Any choice?"

Farrow shook his head. "None."

"Then I'm okay with it."

For a bizarre moment Farrow reached across the desk as if to shake Grant's hand, then abandoned the idea. "It's for the good of the community," the captain said as Grant got up. "And for the good of everybody in this department."

Grant turned to the door.

"And one more thing, Bill," Farrow said, his voice once again almost friendly. "Take the next week off, paid vacation. Gergen insisted on it." He gave a false laugh. "He'll find the money somewhere in the budget. He called it pin money."

Grant nodded without turning around.

"See you in a week, Bill."

Grant opened the door, stepped out, and closed the door behind him.

Without looking at anyone, he walked out of the station and to his car and drove off, heading toward Sagett Road.

Chapter Thirty-five

Corrie marked their second day of walking with an admittedly inaccurate system he had devised. But he decided it would drive him crazy if he couldn't somehow mark the passage of time, as well as distance, so he melded the two and came up with a way to count their progress. He picked out a distant landmark—a clump of bushes, a particular rock, an albedo feature darker than the surrounding landscape—and when they reached it he counted off an hour.

At first he knew he was off—the first landmark, a tall, willowy tree, proved to be much farther away than he thought—but by the end of the second "day" he felt pretty comfortable with his estimations.

At what Corrie determined to be "eight o'clock," he and Reggie stopped to eat and rest for the "night." There had been, as Corrie had guessed, absolutely no change in the sky indicating a solar source of light since they'd arrived here. The sky stayed a uniform sickly yellow, with gray clouds that never seemed to move. The only change of any kind Corrie had noticed was that the dark smudges at the horizon seemed to be growing in number and height. Once he thought he heard a distant rumbling sound, but it had quickly disappeared into the eerie silence that prevailed.

They had picked up plenty of the scallion roots along the way, and Corrie had tried to fashion a crude water carrier from his leather wallet, which hadn't worked but hadn't been needed. They discovered that wherever the scallion bushes were, there was water, too.

Corrie couldn't be sure, but it looked as though the wall in front of the structure they had seen their first day was a little higher in the sky, and therefore closer. But it still looked to be days away.

"So how you feeling, Reggie?" he asked, trying to be cheerful.

She turned her huge black eyes on him; with her gray hair she resembled a miniature little old lady.

"I'm more tired today, Corrie. When are we going to get there?"

He could tell by the fact that she didn't run her sentences on that she really was tired.

"I don't know. We're just going to have to keep going, I guess. I can't see anything else to do."

She was staring blankly at the huge wall in the

distance. "What will we do when we get there? How will we climb it?"

He stared at it himself. Instead of telling her the truth he said, "Don't worry, we'll be just fine."

"Are we dead, Corrie?" She was looking straight at him now.

This time he didn't lie. "I don't know, Reggie."

He noticed that there were tears on her cheeks. "I miss my mom and dad," she said.

"I know. There are people I miss, too. But John said this was what we had to do, so I guess we have to do it."

She covered her eyes with her balled fists. "I don't want to be here!"

He suddenly remembered how young she was, and how much less time she had to get used to the terrible things that had happened.

He sat down beside her and hugged her to him.

"It's all right, Reggie. We're in this together. I have to tell you that I'd be a lot more scared and lonely right now if you weren't with me."

She sniffled and looked up at him. "Really?"

He nodded. "Doesn't it help a little just to have someone else with you?"

"Yes." She buried her face in his side and soon was asleep.

When he was sure she wouldn't wake he lay her gently down and stood up. Sleep was far away for him. He felt restless and angry. They had been here two days and nothing had happened. Supposedly a battle for control of two worlds was raging and there was no evidence of it. It was like the two of them had been dropped on a far planet and forgotten.

Still, he believed what John had told him, that this was the way things had to be done.

He stared at the far wall.

How will *we get up it*—

He blinked—something had detached itself from the near distance and flashed against the yellow-red of the wall in the distance. It was moving sideways and toward him, kicking up a slight trail of dust—

Someone—or something—was approaching.

Marking Reggie's sleeping spot in his mind by memorizing the shapes of the scallion bushes nearby, Corrie set out to meet the approaching figure.

He still could not make it out clearly—either it was too far away or blended too well into the background. If not for the trail it left he would have lost it altogether a half dozen times.

But then it was close enough to resolve into something huge and square, and bearing down on him with great speed.

Fear took hold of him. He almost turned to run back to Reggie, but the thing was already nearly at him. It grew larger, a good twenty feet tall and almost perfectly square. Corrie could not see its form of locomotion, but it suddenly reared up in front of him and stopped dead.

It looked like a slab of stone, perfectly square, a foot or so thick. The dust it had driven up by its flight settled around its base. There were no visible wheels or legs.

Corrie walked around behind it—it was as smooth and flat in back as in front.

"Hello?" Corrie said tentatively.

The slab of stone—it looked something like pink granite—just sat there.

Corrie reached out and touched it.

His hand sunk to the wrist in something as soft as cotton.

Corrie waited for a yelp of pain, but there was only silence from the thing.

"Can you talk?" Corrie asked.

"I can speak," the thing answered suddenly; the voice was so deep and booming that Corrie took a step back. "You are to sleep, and then we will go."

"Who sent you?"

The thing was stone silent.

"Why should we go with you?"

Corrie began to retrace his steps to where Reggie lay sleeping; the thing followed, keeping a constant distance, and stopped a good ten yards from the spot by the scallion bushes.

Corrie lay down on the ground, and found that he was suddenly extremely tired.

He closed his eyes.

His last vision was of the thing, looming over him—

Corrie awoke. Reggie was already awake, yelping with glee like a puppy. Corrie remembered for a moment the strange dream he had had, the huge stone slab which had come rushing out of the desert at him—

He looked up to see Reggie twenty feet in the air, on top of the pink square stone, howling with laughter, bouncing high and then landing on the stone, sinking into it like sponge before being tossed up again.

"He's soft like a stuffed bear!"

The stone said in its booming low voice. "Good morning. Are you ready to travel, or do you need to eat or excrete first?"

Corrie blinked. "Wha—?"

"We should leave soon, if possible."

"I—" Corrie shrugged, went to the clusters of scallion bushes and extracted a fistful of roots, which he stuffed in his pocket. He found the water spot and drank, then returned to stand before the soft monolith.

"Climb up my side, or I will assist you if needed."

"I—" Corrie hesitated, then reached out, grabbing a handful of the soft matter on the smooth side of the stone. It bunched in his hand, allowing him to grip. He did the same with his other hand,

and then sank his feet into the matter and climbed up.

Near the top he hesitated. The entire stone convulsed, throwing him up and over. He found himself on top, Reggie still bouncing happily beside him. It was like resting in foam.

"We will proceed," the monolith announced.

They took off at terrific speed toward the distant wall. And then they accelerated to even greater speed. Corrie found himself clutching the foam to either side of him and digging his heels down into it. He looked at the wall, which now was visibly growing closer and taller. Reggie had stopped bouncing, and sat clutching the foam herself, sitting up and staring in disbelief at the wall.

"Hey!" Corrie called.

There was no answer from their vehicle, only a further acceleration.

"Reggie, hold on as tight as you can!"

The wall rose, and now Corrie could see striations in it, fissures and cracks that towered above them.

It must be at least a mile high, Corrie thought.

As the wall towered, their carrier increased his speed yet again.

"Reggie!" Corrie threw one arm out to cover the girl as the wall rose up impossibly high above them.

Then suddenly there was a huge gap in front of them.

They drove through it.

291

Without slowing down, they were out the other side, rushing down a gentle, impossibly long slope toward the massive structure in the near distance. Their speed decreased. The structure looked naturally man-made—as if a pile of huge stones had dropped into place randomly but made a building that looked planned. There were sheer walls and what looked like parapets and a single massively tall tower with a jagged top.

They grew closer. Their speed lessened even more. Corrie took his arm from Reggie and began to breathe again. He sat up.

He studied the area around the stone building. It was swarming with shapes. They were now into the outer reach of the crowd. Something that looked like a thin, very tall balloon turned to regard them as they went past. There were other shapes of all kinds, twists of cotton candy, boxes, some of them massive, solid looking balls, the cardboard cutout he and Reggie had seen in their mutual dream which had something resembling eyes.

Their vehicle stopped before this creature abruptly.

"You may get down," it boomed, in a voice more command than request.

Corrie helped Reggie climb down, then followed.

The cardboard cutout—up close he looked to be made of something more rough surfaced than cardboard, more like a bubbled sheet of dark glass—regarded them silently for a moment from the great height of his three flat eyes, like the eyes of a flounder fish, then said simply, "Follow."

Their small procession made its way through the silent crowd of strange shapes. Corrie stared up at a pale pink string that rose like a magician's trick rope into the pale gray clouds above. Next to it a squat ovoid resembling a huge blood-red bean, pulsing dully with some hidden heartbeat, crawled along the ground on encircling yellow cilia.

There was a rough gap in the side of the building similar to the one in the rock wall, and they approached it.

The cardboard cutout abruptly announced, "On Earth, I was an African prince." He seemed as startled by the announcement as Corrie. After a pause he appended: "I haven't thought of that since I've been here."

"Yes?"

The cutout stopped and glared down at the two humans with its three blank eyes. "You don't understand. When we arrive here we don't remember those things. We start over. Strange . . ." He stared over their heads into his own thoughts for a moment, then turned around.

"Please come with me."

"What is this place?" Corrie asked.

"It is Samhain's abode, when he is here. Since this battle began we have taken it for our own purposes."

"Doesn't he mind?"

"There is nothing he can do. We are as dead as he is."

They went through the wide gap in the wall. Corrie expected to feel the temperature cool but as when they had passed through the rock wall, the air, the temperature, were exactly constant.

"You okay, Sniffles?"

Reggie was breathing a little shallowly, but she nodded. "Like a weird dream."

"Yes," Corrie agreed.

On the other side of the gap was a wide flat space, which they traversed before coming to a huge set of steps. Without comment the cardboard cutout began to mount them. They were so large that Corrie had to pull Reggie up each step which slowed them down to the point where their host stopped and turned around.

"I apologize, I hadn't realized the difficulty—"

In a blur, the cardboard cutout bent toward them, scooped them up and deposited them beside him in one smooth motion.

There was another landing and then another which they climbed in similar fashion, followed by a final long corkscrew of steps. Then they were out in the open.

The cardboard cutout retreated, leaving them on a flat deck which proved to be the top of the tower. On one side a jagged wall rose up, but on this side, facing the far, blackened horizon, the deck led to a precipice.

Corrie thought they were alone. But when he

pproached the ledge a singular figure resolved out
f the sour light: a tall, thin wisp of smoke. It hung
n the air as if it might dissipate at any moment.

He had the feeling it was studying the far vista.
As he approached, the trail of smoke shifted, ro-
ated toward him—

The smoke figure gasped.

Corrie stopped, Reggie behind him.

"I'm . . . sorry," the figure said. Its voice was
trong but faint, like the voice of someone vibrant
eard from far away. Corrie couldn't help but no-
ice the shock in the voice.

"Is . . . ?"

"It's nothing," the wisp of smoke said. "A memory. Let me see the girl, please."

Corrie stepped aside and motioned Reggie to
ome stand beside him. The wisp of smoke hung
motionless, but there was the faintest sound of
pproval.

"Yes, we were right to include her."

The smoke rope twisted, turning back toward
he vista before them, and whispered, "The two of
ou, please. Come stand beside me."

Corrie edged up next to the smoke rope, draw-
ng Reggie after him. He stopped her a yard from
he edge of the deck, but moved a little closer him-
elf, staring over—

He nearly swooned at the height—it was like be-
ng on a mountaintop.

"Be careful—" the rope cautioned, and Corrie
elt the thinnest of touches as he was urged back.

The rope regarded the horizon.

"That is where it will all end," it said. There was regret and anticipation in the words. "Getting the two of you here was half the battle. The other half has yet to be fought."

"What is it you want us to do?" Corrie asked.

The rope ignored the question. Instead, a thin tendril snaked out from its middle, as a pointer. "That is where the battle rages now. Many have been lost in the last weeks, in anticipation of you getting here." Corrie studied a darker smudge against the low sky; he remembered the black bite out of the sky of his dreams.

Again he asked, "What can we do?" but again the rope creature ignored him.

"We will travel after you rest," the rope said. "The sooner the better. There is water and food below for you. You must be as strong as possible."

The rope creature's thoughts seemed to wander as its words trailed off. Again it turned to regard first Reggie, and then Corrie.

Corrie became uncomfortable under its gaze.

"Such a long time . . ." the rope said.

Corrie looked at the horizon, and then at the creature. Impatience filled him. "Yes, a long time," he said. "You've been plotting to get me here for twenty years, ever since I was seven." He pointed at Reggie. "She's only seven years old, and look what you've done to her."

"We know that. It was necessary."

"Where's John?"

The smoke shifted. "I am John. In your world, you saw me as a familiar creature, which was the only way I could appear to you. In this world, this how your eyes perceive me." He regarded Corrie for a long moment. "Truly remarkable . . ."

Corrie's tone softened, but he was adamant this time, "What is it you need us to do?"

The smoke that was John regarded him for a very long time. Then it shifted back to view the battle at the horizon.

"We need you to die," it said, in a whisper.

Chapter Thirty-six

Corrie Phaeder's house was empty and unguarded. There was crime scene tape across the front entry, but Grant ignored it. He deftly used a credit card to open the door and entered.

Would have made a good criminal, he thought, and smiled grimly.

The house was quiet as midnight. Grant's shoes on the creaky stairs were the only sound as he climbed to the second floor.

Corrie's room was pretty much untouched. It had probably been lightly tossed by a uniform who didn't know what he was doing or looking for.

Grant stood in the middle of the floor.

He didn't know what he had expected to feel— some energy, some force, some indication that Phaeder and the little girl were safe and alive.

Halloween was a memory. The front of Corrie's house had been well egged, since Phaeder had been busy with other things rather than giving out candy. The weather today, on November 1st, was anything but beautiful. The deep blue sky and perfect chilled temperature of yesterday had been replaced by low gray clouds and chilly dampness. It looked as if it might rain any minute.

Grant did a routine search of the room, if for no other reason than to keep busy. There was little of interest. In the adjacent room he found the camera and tripod which he had knocked aside yesterday in his haste to keep the hornets out.

Grant noticed that the window in the room looked out on a cornfield across Sagett River. A scarecrow hung on a post in the middle of it.

Grant picked up the camera and looked through it. The telephoto lens was sharply focused, without his adjustment, on the scarecrow.

It had the head of a pumpkin.

As he watched the head moved, the eyes lit up and seemed to look straight at him—

He blinked, looked away, then looked back through the camera's viewfinder.

The pumpkin was inert, guarding late golden corn.

Grant put the camera down on the floor and left the house.

The river was easy to cross, but when he reached the cornfield he lost his bearings. The scarecrow was no longer visible over the tops of the dried stalks. When he pushed his way into the first row and then the second he quickly lost all sense of direction.

There was a rustle to his left, as something moved past him.

"Follow me, Detective Grant."

John's head briefly appeared. Grant followed the scarecrow through the ranks of corn until they were in the center of the field in a small clearing. The empty pole John had been mounted on stood bare, a mute testament.

John turned to face him.

His pumpkin face was rotting, the smile twisted lopsided and curling inward. There were white worms crawling in and out of the eye holes.

John said, "This is the last time I can speak to you." His voice sounded faint and distracted. "I wanted you to know that Corrie and Regina have reached my world."

"They're dead?"

"Very much alive, Detective. They're resting now."

"And then?"

"And then we'll see. I thought I owed you a debt of thanks for protecting them. I thought I might pay you back in some small way."

Grant waited.

"In my world," John went on, "we remember none of our time here on Earth. But the presence of Corrie and Regina has triggered memory in those who have been near them. It has something to do with the fact that they straddle two planes of existence. They've brought a bit of Earth with them, I suppose." He paused. "I wanted you to know that your wife Rose is with us."

Grant's heart skipped a beat. "Rose . . ."

"If all goes well, she will be fine."

"Take me back with you," Grant said. "I'll help you. I'll do anything I can—"

"You've already done more than you realize, Detective Grant. I hope what I've told you has brought you some comfort. If you go to the farm where they passed over to us, you can wait there. I will be soon. If things work out against us, it will make no difference where you are.

"Pray for us, if you like, Mr. Grant."

"But you said—"

A smile creased the ruined pumpkin face. "I said I didn't know, Mr. Grant. I still don't. But don't you feel that some other power must be behind all of this, even if it shows no overt interest?"

"I don't know . . ."

The pumpkin figure put a hand on Grant's shoulder. "As I said, neither do I . . ."

Before Grant's eyes, John disintegrated, breaking into a moldering pile of decay and then, as if in a movie, dried dust.

Grant looked at the empty pole. His hands were shaking.

Chapter Thirty-seven

"Time to be going."

Corrie was having the most wonderful dream. He was four years old. His mother had taken him to the park and was pushing him on a swing. He gave a whoop of joy at each apex, and as he swung back down to her she followed the swing's arc up with her hands and gave him a solid push forward, saying, "That's my boy!" each time. He went higher and higher, feeling his stomach rise as he hit the height of his arc and then fall as he dropped back. He was as happy as he had ever been, and it was all the more wonderful because it had really happened.

He awoke to see John looming over him, a statuesque length of smoke.

"It's time," John said.

Corrie sat up, rubbing his eyes. Reggie, yawning, was doing the same next to him. They had slept on the soft red rock creature that brought them here, who had lain down to form a remarkably comfortable bed.

Suddenly Corrie fully remembered where he was, and a hollowness filled him.

"Are you ready?" John asked.

"Will I ever be?"

Corrie had the feeling that John was smiling humorlessly.

"We must go."

Corrie and Regina followed the column of smoke out of their private room and onto the flat deck of the tall tower. They walked to the edge. Below them was spread a multitude of strange shapes. Corrie knew, though he couldn't tell by their bizarre appearances—curlicues, rectangles, ovals, pillars, squat round buttons, tall boxy shapes of all hues—that they were staring up at him.

They were utterly silent.

In the distance, the black sky reached up from the horizon. A distant thumping sound like that of giant machinery could barely be heard. As Corrie watched, there was a tearing sound as another patch of black ate up the sky.

John spoke to the crowd below: "This is the time of the last battle. Soon we will know. But be aware that without these two friends from Earth, we would have no chance. What they have given up to come here is more than we can imagine. Each of us had a full time on Earth; these two did not. Their sacrifice is our blessing."

Corrie had expected some sort of cheer. Instead, there was something even more chilling and affecting.

As one, the entire crowd of thousands of strange shapes bowed themselves silently against the ground.

"Come," John said, and Corrie and Regina followed him, with some difficulty, down the huge steps, eventually to the ground floor.

They walked out of the building and the massive crowd, no longer prostrate, parted to let them pass. There was an eerie quiet. Only the thumping, which grew louder by the minute, broke the silence. As they moved through the massed shapes a few joined them, falling in behind: the cardboard cutout they had met the day before, and two others—a pale green star-shaped creature and one that resembled a balloon.

Soon they had left the huge building and the crowd of onlookers behind.

They were back in the desert, with no discernible road in front of them.

"Do we walk?" Corrie asked.

John said calmly, "We would never get there."

The balloon moved up as if on cue, and John said, "Climb in."

Below the balloon shape was something like a wide seat. Corrie made himself comfortable on it. John's smoky shape compacted, and he settled himself next to Corrie.

Almost at once the balloon rose. Corrie's stomach dropped out from beneath him, and once more he was reminded of his dream.

He looked down to see Reggie sitting in the middle of the green starfish, which was flying over the ground. He heard a yelp of pleasure. The cardboard cutout flapped along beside it like a bizarre manta ray.

"Tell me what to expect," Corrie said.

Already, as they drew closer to the edge of the world, the sky was growing darker in front of them. The thumping became more insistent. Corrie could feel it in his chest, a deep measured throb.

"The Dark One is eating away this world piece by piece," John said. "He is forcing his own world, which is nothingness, into this one. Three quarters of this way station is already gone.

"You will have to face him on the ground."

Corrie felt his stomach tighten.

"When this campaign began, we of course tried to face him ourselves. Those who did simply disappeared. They turned from something into . . . nothing."

"What makes you think I can do any better?"

John was silent. "That is the hard part. You were prepared for this long ago, Corrie, because, coming from your world into this one, and still being alive, you hold certain powers of negation over the Dark One. If he destroys my world, then he can move into yours. But he cannot deal directly with your world. You are a line he cannot cross. He will try, because he must, but when he does he will be thrown back into his own realm and shut out of this one. His only hope was to pass through this place directly to Earth. But . . ."

"I'll die when he tries."

"Yes."

"And disappear like the others."

John was silent, and then said, "We think so."

Corrie looked down at Reggie. "And what about her? Is she the backup, in case I fail?"

John was silent. "No."

Corrie found himself getting angry. "I won't let anything happen to her. If I have to die then let it happen. But send her back to Earth and her parents."

"You don't understand."

Corrie waited, but John said nothing.

Finally, the figure next to him said, "*You* are the backup, Corrie. She is the one who must face the Dark One, and be annihilated."

Corrie was speechless.

"It is hard for me to explain," John said. "Though you were prepared for years, it was discovered when the time drew close for this battle that you . . . might fail."

"How?"

"The Dark One . . . may be able to use certain things against you to weaken you. Reggie, it was discovered, is much stronger and will be able to withstand these . . . temptations."

Corrie was stunned. "I won't let anything happen to Reggie."

"You don't have a choice. She is the one who must meet the Dark One, or we all will perish."

Corrie looked down at Reggie, who was still shouting "Wheee!" as the starfish she road flew over the desert below.

"You can't do this! She doesn't know! And after all that time, all those years and the things I went through, you tell me I'm not *good* enough to help you?"

Corrie felt a light touch on his shoulder, which reminded him of the first time he had met John, by the cornfield after he returned to Orangefield. It seemed a thousand years ago. The pillar of smoke had moved nearer, and a thin tendril of its matter was formed into a delicate hand with thin smoky fingers.

"Corrie, I know this is hard. But this is how it must be."

"I won't let it happen. I promised to take care of her."

John said quietly, "I also have a selfish reason for being thankful this is the way things turned out."

Corrie was still staring down at Reggie.

"Do you remember the effect you had when you arrived among us?" John asked. "Those of us who came into contact with you remembered their former lives on Earth."

Corrie said nothing.

"So did I," John said.

Still, Corrie was silent.

"I'm your mother, Corrie."

Corrie stiffened.

"I remembered yesterday. It was like a lance through me. But it's true."

"My mother . . ."

Corrie turned to stare at the thing next to him, the thing he had known as John: who had helped him into this world and who now told him that the little girl who had been dragged along with him had to die.

"You see, if it's necessary for Reggie to face the Dark One, I will be able to keep you alive. You will be safe. Otherwise, you might disappear forever. Now that I know who I am, I could not bear to lose you again."

"It's still not fair to her!"

"This is how it must be. When I first came here to Samhain's domain, twelve Earth years ago, I felt I had a special calling to help you. I didn't realize why. There were others"—she indicated the cardboard cutout, still driving itself over the desert below like a landlocked ray—"already doing the work. They had been preparing you since you were seven. But I felt compelled to help. Now I know why. In a way, I didn't have a choice, Corrie."

In the distance, the sky grew taller and blacker and more empty, and the *thump-thump* grew in Corrie's chest like a dagger being thrust there.

The world was black. Above them, towering like a line of massive thunderheads, the fabric of the world disappeared. They hovered, and Corrie

looked down: the desert was there below him, bu
a little ahead it disappeared into a ragged black
emptiness. There was this world, and then one
step further on there was . . . absolutely nothing.

He was reminded of the ancient Earth explorer.
who feared that if they sailed west from Europe
they would fall off the edge of the world.

There was a hollow, massive *boom*. Below the
balloon the desert disappeared. There was no
falling of sand and rock. One moment the pale
land was there, and then suddenly it had vanished
Corrie felt a faint wash of bone-chilling dry cold
move past him.

He leaned out to peer into the new darkness
which faced them like a wall. The yellow haze and
gray clouds of the atmosphere ended as if snipped
off with a pair of scissors. In the blackness, there
was no movement, no sound, no hint of habitation
or life.

Another thunderous thumping *boom*, and they
were rocked back by the advance of the black wall

Beside Corrie his mother made a motion, and
the balloon slowly settled to the ground. They
stepped from it. Reggie's starfish lay still, and she
was helped down and ran to Corrie.

She was no longer laughing. "Corrie, I'm
scared!"

Corrie drew her close and said, "Don't worry
Reggie. Like I told you, we're in this together."

Reggie suddenly pointed. "Look!"

Corrie looked to his left. Something was moving swiftly over the desert toward them, a wide, faint cloud of vapor that compacted and coalesced as it grew closer.

"*Samhain,*" Corrie's mother whispered.

The cloud reared up in front of them, took shape into a frightening ghoulish face ten yards high, a flat wide oval with empty eyes and a huge mouth.

Reggie held Corrie tightly. He could feel her trembling.

"You cannot harm them here," Corrie's mother said.

"True," Samhain's voice boomed. "But, now that you're close, I can deal with *you*—"

Howling with rage, the face rose up. A body— thin torso, impossibly long arms, taloned fingers— formed beneath it.

With a sudden movement Samhain's clawed hands lashed out, sweeping John and the starfish that had borne Reggie into the empty darkness.

"*Mother!*"

There was a single muffled cry, cut off, as the two shapes disappeared into the blackness.

Samhain reared up over Corrie.

"I can take the girl back, now. Give her to me and I'll return her safely to Earth."

Corrie smiled grimly at the huge figure. "Even you know I'll fail?"

"I'll take you both back, if you wish."

"Then no one faces the Dark One, and you win."

A wind was rising around Samhaim. Corrie

could feel the ground beneath him begin to tremble. The blackness in front of him crept forward and above, the black nothingness arched over in a wave, making the sky disappear all at once.

"Corrie! I'm so scared!" Reggie cried.

Samhain was looking up in wonder, his mouth open in awe.

"Dark One . . ." he said.

The wave rose and widened. There was an impossibly deep booming sound. It was like nothing Corrie had ever heard, like the rending of the heavens themselves. He lifted Reggie and held her away from him. She was crying hysterically. Her black eyes were growing blacker and deeper and wider as the wall of nothingness closed in all around them like a prison.

A voice like thunder proclaimed, *"ALL OF YOU WILL SOON BE WIPED FROM THE FACE OF THE UNIVERSE."*

"Remember me," Corrie whispered to Reggie, then he turned to face Samhain.

"Take her back!" he shouted, and flung the girl at Samhain.

Then he leaped into the nothingness—

The booming ceased in an instant. All sound was gone, and light, and time. Corrie felt nothing—there was no ground beneath his feet, no air to breathe, no wind, no taste, touch, odor, sight.

He did not even feel suspended.

He was surrounded on all sides by—*nothing*.

"So it is you, after all," a voice said. It did not come from any particular direction, and it was not in his head—he just heard it, as if it had come out of nowhere. It was oddly flat, and calm, and hateful.

It sounded pleased.

"Yes," he said.

"They prepared you a long time. But you know nothing."

"Then I know you."

"The girl was stronger. Yet you came instead."

"I wanted her to live."

"Nothing will live. After our meeting, everything will be gone. Every scrap of life on your world. Already, death itself is gone."

"Why do you hate us?"

A pause. "I don't hate."

"You hate life."

"It's the opposite of what I am. Creation leads to chaos. It is messy. Without creation, the Universe was a placid place."

"Who created creation?"

A longer pause. "No one knows."

"And yet you try to destroy it."

"Samhain has found you interesting creatures. That is because he is inextricably linked with you. Your deaths give him life, and meaning. Your questions mean nothing."

"Because you are nothing."

"Yes."

313

"If you are nothing, how can you speak?"

"Because I wish to. I am nothingness itself, not a creature of it."

"How can I stop you?"

There was the longest pause yet. "You've already failed."

"Why?"

"Because you're still alive."

"You haven't moved from Samhain's world into my own, have you?"

"No."

"Why not?"

"Because . . . you are here."

"Preventing you?"

There was silence.

He knew the Dark One had withdrawn—though there was no change in his surroundings, no change in temperature or air pressure, no difference in his blank surroundings.

He knew he was alone.

And then he saw a light.

He moved toward it, though he didn't feel himself walking. There was no sense of movement. The light grew closer. It resolved into a vertical rectangle, a door, and suddenly he was through it and standing in a room.

He could breathe again, and smell, and taste his own sweat, and feel his feet on the floor beneath him.

He studied his surroundings. The door he had passed through was now closed, and there was another door in front of him. The room was a cube about ten feet on a side, made of steady light. He stood on something that felt like a floor.

"Choose," the Dark One said.

The door in front of him opened. He saw a vast red plain, a multitude of motionless figures. They were gauzy, barely discernible, human-shaped. A sea of moans emanated from their unmoving features. Their eyes were fixed on nothing, pleading.

One of them, close to the door, was his mother.

"This is how they appeared when they were alive on Earth," the Dark One said. "For the moment, I thought it best to preserve them."

"As a weapon."

"Yes. Make your choice. If you walk toward them, you will die. If you go back through the door you came through, you will not die."

"You'll destroy everything. My world and theirs."

"Yes. But *you* will live. I will allow that. I will let you live forever."

Now he knew why his mother and the others had wanted to send Reggie instead of him.

She would never have been tempted by such an offer.

As he was tempted . . .

"My life for . . . everything."

"Yes. Perhaps this will help you decide."

Suddenly he saw the death that awaited him if he stepped onto the red plain. His limbs torn from his body, his living heart bursting in front of his own eyes, his screams of agony echoing in his own ears.

"Do you want to die?"

He fell to his knees.

The room contracted. There was a door at his back, and one, closed now, directly in front of him. He felt the cold breath from the door in front of him, and the warmth of the one behind, the caress of what felt like loving arms on him.

He looked back through the other door, now. He was on his own Earth, with the warmth of the sun eternally on his face, a cool breeze and the finest of everything. He had only to wish a thing and it would happen—the best food, the finest entertainment, simulacra of women and animals and anyone from history he wanted to meet. If he wanted to race a car, it would be there, in front of him. If he wanted to fly a plane, the same. Casinos, the best hotels in the history of Earth. Any historical period he wanted to visit, it would be recreated for him down to the smallest detail.

Then, once more, he saw what awaited him through the other door: the horrible wrenching of limb from limb, the tearing of his tendons from their joints, his fingers from his hands, one by one snapped away from his body . . .

This is why they wanted Reggie.

This is why they didn't want me.

He felt his bowels contract, fell to the ground, hugging himself in a fetal position.

His hand reached out to the safe door and he felt its warmth emanating toward him.

"*Choose,*" the voice of the Dark One said, now

oothing, helping him to make the choice for him-
elf, what did it matter anyway—

His hand brushed the warm door, and then with
a wrenching cry he threw himself at the other
loor, driving himself through it, listening to his
own suddenly unbearable screams—

Chapter Thirty-eight

Grant had been dozing on and off for hours in Riley Gates's old lawn chair, facing the pumpkin field, his revolver in his lap, when he felt the ground shake.

It was as if some underground god had punched upward at him.

"Holy shit."

The ground heaved again, nearly throwing him out of the chair.

He jumped up, studying the horizon. The world outside of Riley's farm seemed normal enough. The waning moon had traversed the sky and now sank toward oblivion in the west.

It would be light in an hour or so.

Again, the ground trembled.

He thought of what John had told him, about the end of the world, and a tight fist of fear formed in his stomach—

Grant was thrown back as a geyser of rock and soil was thrown into the air.

Brilliant light flared from the ground in front of him, and he was momentarily blinded.

He stared straight ahead, expecting the sky to explode, as his vision slowly returned—

There was a whimpering figure lying huddled on the ground, next to an open pit.

Its hair was white as ash.

Grant got up slowly, unsteadily pointing his 9mm.

"Corrie?" he asked tentatively.

The figure sat up, covering its head, shaking like a leaf.

Grant slowly approached.

It was the little girl, Reggie Bright.

Grant put his gun down and lifted her up.

Her face was streaked with tears, but otherwise she seemed all right.

Grant hugged her close and asked, "Reggie, where's Corrie?"

She looked at him with her large brown eyes and then buried her face in his shoulder, crying.

"It's okay, Reggie," Grant soothed. "I'm going to take you to your mom and dad."

Grant walked off as the sun began to light the east with dawn.

Chapter Thirty-nine

ohn awoke in the desert. A familiar sickly yellow ky scudded with low unmoving gray clouds was verhead.

Next to him, the thing shaped like a cardboard utout was stirring.

Other shapes around him were doing the same.

He turned his smoky form to regard the stone tructure in the distance. He could just make out he familiar form of Samhain on the tower ledge. Jo doubt the Lord of the Dead was regarding 'ith interest the vast scene below him.

The desert plains were covered from horizon to orizon with figures.

His kingdom back to normal, John thought.

"The human Corrie Phaeder saved us all," the hing that looked like a cardboard cutout said.

"Yes," John answered. There was a vague ache in

him, but he could not place it. There had bee
something about the young man, something eve
more special than his role in their salvation . . .

"Do you remember anything?" he asked th
cardboard cutout.

"About what?"

"About . . . Earth. Your life there."

The cutout regarded his question, then an
swered with finality. "No."

John was silent.

And then, Samhain was before him.

Something about the way he held himself, th
vague smoky sheet that formed and reformec
making his ghostly face, his shimmering bod
made John feel that Samhain was regarding hir
with bemusement.

He said: "You were victorious. I congratulat
you."

"Won't your master be angry with you?"

"I will deal with him when I must. We hav
had . . . discussions before. They are not as loud c
as dangerous as you might think. In a way I'm gla
things turned out this way. Eternal rest in the forr
of nothingness was not as appealing in the end as
thought it would be. But it still may happen . .
someday."

"And I will do what I must to prevent it."

"Someone like you, perhaps. But not you. You
time here is finished."

"What do you mean?" John asked.

Even as he finished the sentence he saw that

great change was coming over the world. The sky was turning to another, deeper color, almost blue. In one section a whirlpool had formed a hole—a bright, fiery color in its center. And the shapes were rising from the ground around him toward it.

Suddenly, he felt light as air as he watched the cardboard cutout soar into the air and away.

"It is a natural thing," Samhain said. "This, as you know, is but a way station. It is time to make room here for the newly dead."

"Corrie . . . ?" John asked.

Samhain shook his head. "He is not among them."

John was in the air now, moving up and away from Samhain.

"Good-bye," he said.

To his vast surprise Samhain smiled wryly, and gave a sort of salute.

"You were an interesting one," he said. "And so was your son."

"My son?" John said.

And then Samhain was a speck below, and John moved toward the light—

John felt himself rushing toward another place. Only now he was no longer John, and he was no longer a wisp of smoke. He suddenly knew his real name: Grace, and knew that he was a woman. The tunnel of illumination widened into a bright opening. Behind it was somewhere she couldn't quite make out, but that was resolving into something completely new. A landscape of—

There was a figure blocking her way, which held out its hand to her as she drew close.

She knew the smile on the face.

She felt his fingers close around her own.

"Mother," he said.

Epilogue

You've failed me again, Samhain.

Yes. And . . .

And I myself failed, as you were about to point out.

Yes, my Lord. As I've told you, these humans are strange, resilient creatures.

I was very close to stripping every speck of life from that miserable planet. I will do it yet.

Yes, my Lord . . .

Do I detect a note of your vile levity? Do you think I'm unaware that you hurried along that last group from your little way station so that I couldn't demand vengeance against them?

There was very little I could do in that regard, as you know, my Lord. My powers, what little there are of them, only work on Earth. You did have the lot of them yourself—

I thought it best to hold them in reserve.

And . . . still the young man did not choose to save himself.

Once again, interesting creatures—

If you say so.

What will you do now, my Lord?

I am brooding. But thinking, also. Perhaps next time a more direct approach. A personal visit . . .

You can do that?

I can do more than you know, Samhain. That is why you are my servant, and not the reverse. It will take all of my power, and much time for preparation.

There's always another Halloween . . .

RICHARD LAYMON

SAVAGE

Whitechapel, November 1888: Jack the Ripper is hard at work. He's safe behind locked doors in a one-room hovel with his unfortunate victim, Mary Kelly. With no need to hurry for once, he takes his time gleefully eviscerating the young woman. He doesn't know that a fifteen-year-old boy is cowering under Mary's bed....

Trevor Bentley's life would never be the same after that night. What he saw and heard would have driven many men mad. But for Trevor it was the beginning of a quest, an obsession to stop the most notorious murderer in history. The killer's trail of blood will lead Trevor from the fog-shrouded alleys of London to the streets of New York and beyond. But Trevor will not stop until he comes face to face with the ultimate horror.

ISBN 10: 0-8439-5751-4
ISBN 13: 978-0-8439-5751-8